# "We'd Do Best To Keep Any Personal Involvement To A Minimum,"

Susannah told Kane.

"You were the one who kissed me."

"To teach you a lesson."

"That you kiss like a seductress? I already knew that."

She blinked. A seductress? Her? With her too-large thighs and wild hair? Was he making fun of her? She stared at him, but saw hunger rather than derision in his blue eyes.

Apparently Kane was as attracted to her as she was to him. And as unhappy about it. It was a startling discovery. Kind of like finding out that the keg you were sitting on was filled with dynamite.

Dear Reader:

Welcome to Silhouette Desire - provocative, compelling, contemporary love stories written by and for today's woman. These are stories to treasure.

Each and every Silhouette Desire is a wonderful romance in which the emotional and the sensual go hand in hand. When you open a Desire, you enter a whole new world - a world that has, naturally, a perfect hero just waiting to whisk you away! A Silhouette Desire can be light-hearted or serious, but it will always be satisfying.

We hope you enjoy this Desire today - and will go on to enjoy many more.

Please write to us:

Jane Nicholls
Silhouette Books
PO Box 236
Thornton Road
Croydon
Surrey
CR9 3RU

# A Wife in Time

## CATHIE LINZ

SILHOUETTE
Desire

First published in Great Britain 1996
by Silhouette Books, Eton House, 18-24 Paradise Road,
Richmond, Surrey TW9 1SR

© Cathie L. Baumgardner 1995

Silhouette, Silhouette Desire and Colophon are
Trade Marks of Harlequin Enterprises II B.V.

ISBN 0 373 05958 2

22-9603

Made and printed in Great Britain

## CATHIE LINZ

left her career in a university law library to become the best-selling author of numerous contemporary romances. An avid romance reader herself, Cathie enjoys hearing from readers; you can write to her at P.O. Box 16, Westmont, IL 60559, United States of America.

Cathie often uses humorous mishaps from her own trips as inspiration for her stories—she got the idea for this time-travel romance while visiting the Davenport House in Savannah. After travelling, Cathie is always glad to get back home to her two cats, her trusty word processor and her hidden cache of cookies!

### Other Silhouette Books by Cathie Linz

*Silhouette Desire*

Change of Heart
A Friend in Need
As Good as Gold
Adam's Way
Smiles
Handyman
Smooth Sailing
Flirting with Trouble
Midnight Ice
Bridal Blues

This book is dedicated to Desire Senior Editor
Lucia Macro, with much thanks for letting me play in
the nineteenth century!
Additional thanks go to Judy Ann Newton for the early
encouragement, talented historical romance author
Linda Wiatr for checking my research, and to the staff
at Downers Grove Public Library for all the historical
nonfiction interlibrary loans.

# One

"Hey, you! Hold it right there! I want to talk to you!"

Susannah Hall ignored the loudly spoken order, certain it couldn't possibly be directed at *her*. In fact, Susannah felt a bit sorry for the poor soul to whom it *was* directed, for the man's command was driven by enough anger to fuel a fleet of jets for a week. A second later she dismissed the man and his anger from her thoughts. She had enough things to worry about.

Although Susannah had been an editor for almost five years now, this was her first time attending the huge American Publishing Convention, taking place in Savannah this year. Her recent promotion to senior editor at McPhearson Publishing meant that she was now expected to attend this bigger-than-life trade show.

From the moment she'd first walked into the convention center earlier that morning, she'd felt like a kid at the circus, surrounded by hype and hoopla. But now, midafternoon hunger pangs had forced her to leave McPhearson's display booth in search of the convention center's cafeteria.

"I said I want to talk to you!" the furious male voice repeated, this time from directly behind her.

Years of living in New York City had Susannah pivoting in her tracks, her huge purse automatically held at the ready should she need to use it in self-defense. The man and his anger were just a little too close for comfort.

He was tall, had dark ruffled hair, and he radiated fury. She'd never seen him before in her life.

Looking around, Susannah was reassured by the presence of the crowd despite the fact that, like water in a stream, the people simply flowed on around them, paying them little heed. But then this was a crowd in single-minded pursuit of the almighty buck, as millions of dollars' worth of transactions were in progress at this convention.

Keeping a cautious grip on her large bag just in case, Susannah addressed the angry stranger. "Are you talking to me?" she demanded.

"Damn right, I'm talking to you," the man confirmed with a growl.

"Shouting was actually closer to the truth," Susannah noted frostily. "What seems to be the problem, Mr.—" She paused to read the name tag that everyone attending this convention was required to wear. Kane Wilder. The name fit, Susannah decided. The man's behavior was certainly wilder than normal or acceptable. "What's the problem, Mr. Wilder?"

"*You're* the problem," Kane Wilder replied, openly glaring at her.

She frowned, unable to imagine what she could have done to have so irritated this man, a man she'd never even met before. "I have no idea what you're talking about," she told him bluntly.

"I'm talking about my brother, Chuck, and the fact that he's threatened to leave his wife because of you."

Stunned, Susannah blinked at Kane. "Excuse me?"

"No, I won't excuse you. There's no excuse for what you've done!"

"I think you've made a mistake of some kind, Mr. Wilder," she began in a conciliatory tone of voice when he interrupted her.

"The only person who has made a mistake is you, Ms. Hall. You *are* Susannah Hall, right? Senior editor at McPhearson Publishing, right?"

"That's right."

"So now you're pretending you don't know my brother? Is that your game?"

"It's no game, Mr. Wilder."

"Playing bedroom games with a younger, married man is exactly the kind of cheap ploy a Mata Hari like you would play."

Mata Hari? Her? Susannah didn't know whether to be insulted or complimented. She couldn't imagine anyone further from the image of a seductress. Her hair was too long and too curly, her figure too full. She knew her eyes and her thighs were both too big. Her taste in clothes was too romantic and soft, although the sky blue suit she wore now was pretty businesslike.

Everyone knew that Mata Hari types were slinky, confident and ruthless. Susannah was a passionate dreamer. The worst that could be said about her was she could be aloof. And when crossed she'd once been called a "tough cookie."

But a Mata Hari? No way. The man was clearly off his rocker.

"My brother's name is Chuck Wilder. Charles Wilder," Kane continued as if speaking to a two-year-old. "Ring any bells or are you fooling around with so many men you've lost count?"

His last stinging comment didn't really sink in as she focused on the first part of his statement. "Are you talking about Charles, the intern at my office?" Susannah had never paid attention to the young man's surname before. He was just "Charles the Intern." One of them, anyway. McPhearson had four at the present time.

"That's right. And you've been teaching him plenty, haven't you?" Kane noted caustically.

"Well, yes, that's what he's there for. To learn."

"Would it have mattered to you if you had known he was married?" Kane demanded.

"Well, no, not really," Susannah admitted. Although most of their interns were still single—and in their junior year of college—it wasn't a requirement for entrance into the internship program.

"Listen, I'm only going to say this once," he bit out. "Stay away from my brother."

"A little hard to do since he works for me," Susannah noted wryly.

"Then fire him."

"I'll do no such thing. Besides, he's an intern. He can't be fired. He's not a paid employee. Look, I'm sorry to hear your brother is having marital difficulties, but I fail to see what that has to do with me."

"Lady, you take the cake! You don't think your having an affair with him might have something to do with his marital problems?"

"An affair?" Susannah repeated in astonishment. Now she *knew* Kane Wilder was off his rocker. "No way!" It was too ridiculous to even contemplate. Sure, she'd had lunch with Charles a few times, but that certainly didn't qualify as an affair! There had never been a hint of any impropriety— Well, there *was* that one time in the copying room two weeks ago when he'd brushed up against her. At the time, she'd thought she'd been imagining things. Now she was quickly reassessing that conclusion.

It made Susannah very uneasy to think that Charles might have had a crush on her and she hadn't even noticed. A crush so intense that he was threatening to leave his wife over it. Things like that didn't happen to her, which was no doubt why she hadn't recognized the signs earlier.

"Look, Mr. Wilder," she began. "Your brother clearly has a problem—"

"Oh, sure, put the blame on him," Kane retorted.

"He *is* the one who's married," she reminded him.

"And you're the one who went after him—a *much* younger man."

Stung, Susannah said, "He's not *that* much younger!"

"You're old enough to know better."

"So is he. Not that anything happened, because it didn't," she quickly clarified before going on to bluntly say, "Your brother is lying if he told you that he's having an affair with me."

"Really?"

"Yes, really."

"And I'm supposed to just take your word for it, is that it?"

Susannah nodded emphatically.

"The word of a woman I've just met over the word of a brother I've helped raise, the brother who has never told a lie in his life."

"Well, when he decided to start, he sure started with a big one," she countered. "Because the claim that the two of us are somehow romantically involved is ludicrous."

"I see. So you're merely sexually—not romantically—involved with him, is that it?"

"No, that's not it! My relationship with your younger brother has been strictly professional."

"*Strictly* professional?" he questioned. "Meaning you never met with him privately. You treated him as you did all your other co-workers?"

Susannah couldn't stop the flash of guilt that shadowed her face.

"I knew it," Kane said, looking at her as if she were something the cat had dragged in.

Susannah's patience was rapidly running out. "No, you don't know anything! Okay," she acknowledged, "so I may have taken him more under my wing than I have with some of the other interns. But that doesn't mean that I'm having an affair with him. Not by any stretch of the imagination!"

"And why do you suppose my brother would lie about something like this?" Kane asked coldly.

"I have no idea. You'd have to ask *him* that question. Maybe you misunderstood what he told his wife," Susannah suggested.

"I didn't misunderstand what he told *me*," Kane retorted.

"I can't believe he made up such a ridiculous story," Susannah said with perplexed frown. "Surely he realized he'd be caught in a lie of this proportion?"

"My point exactly," Kane agreed with a pleasant smile that conveyed mockery rather than humor. "It would be pretty foolish of him to lie about something like this."

"That doesn't mean he's telling the truth, however," Susannah quickly maintained. "When I get back to New York, I'll clearly have to talk with him."

"Another little talk at your place?"

"He's never been to my place." She paused, remembering the time she'd stayed home to read manuscripts and he'd brought over a contract she'd needed to authorize. "Okay, so maybe he was at my place. Once. For five minutes. Maybe fifteen. I offered him a cup of coffee."

"I'm sure you did. Along with a little sympathy about his unsupportive wife."

"I didn't even know he had a wife!"

"Well, now that you do, you can break it off."

"How many times do I have to tell you, there's nothing to break off," she said through gritted teeth.

"You can tell me until you're blue in the face. That doesn't mean I believe a word you say. But believe *me* when I tell you that I'm not about to stand by and watch my brother get hurt by a—"

"Mata Hari like me," Susannah sarcastically completed. "I get the picture, Mr. Wilder. And I'll be expecting an apology from you in writing when this misunderstanding is cleared up."

He stared at her in astonishment. "You've got some nerve, lady."

"Oh, so now you think I'm a lady," she said mockingly. "Funny, you didn't act like it a moment ago when you accused me of seducing your brother. If it weren't so absurd, I'd be highly insulted. As it is, I'll chalk your incredibly rude behavior up to male hysteria.''

''Those two words are mutually exclusive.''

''Not in your case,'' Susannah noted sweetly before turning on her heel and marching into the sanctuary of the women's bathroom.

''I'm not done talking to you!'' Kane bellowed from outside the door.

''Do you know if there's another way out of here?'' Susannah asked a woman in the bathroom.

''That door over there leads to the hallway outside the exhibition area.''

''Great. Thanks.'' She made a beeline for that exit. Her little run-in with Kane Wilder had just taken up fifteen of the thirty minutes she had for lunch. Standing in the long line at the convention center's cafeteria ate up another ten. Meanwhile, Susannah still hadn't eaten a thing.

She grabbed an apple and an anemic-looking green salad, all the while lecturing herself on how she should have handled Kane. She wasn't happy with the way he'd put her on the defensive. She should have stopped him in his verbal tracks the second he started making his ridiculous accusations.

Stashing her purchases in her oversize purse, Susannah hurried back to her employer's display booth. She never did get around to eating, as a rush of people stopped by the booth. As one of the representatives of McPhearson Publishing, it was her job to answer any questions booksellers might have about the line of books McPhearson published.

Smiling at conventioneers as they passed by the booth, Susannah couldn't help wondering if Charles the Intern had told his ridiculous story to anyone else, aside from his wife and his brother. Specifically, had he told any of her co-workers? And if he did, surely they hadn't believed him, had they? Not that she was about to come out and ask. But perhaps she could make a few discreet inquiries....

She started with Roy, the head of Marketing. "So what's your impression of our batch of interns this year?" she asked him during a lull in the action.

"They seem okay," Roy replied. "Is it just me or do they seem to get wetter behind the ears each year?"

Susannah was tempted to ask about Charles specifically but then reconsidered, realizing her inquiry might only raise further speculation. The best thing to do would be to confront Charles when she returned to the office Monday morning—to go directly to the source...and kill him!

She grinned, making a passing sales rep pause and look at her twice. Of course, Susannah had no intention of doing Kane's precious baby brother any bodily harm, but she'd certainly make him wish he'd thought twice about dragging *her* reputation through the mud.

She pumped Roy from Marketing again. "Ever heard of Wilder Enterprises?"

"Aren't they that hotshot company on the forefront of the new CD-ROM technology?"

"CD-what technology? Speak English here, Roy."

"I forgot I was speaking to a technophobic editor afraid to turn on the computer on her own desk."

"I'm not afraid to turn it on," Susannah calmly denied. "We have an understanding. I don't bother it, and it doesn't bother me."

"It could make your workload a lot easier."

"I know I'll have to learn how to use it eventually," she admitted. "But I'm not in any rush since the rest of the office isn't hooked up yet."

"It will be by the end of the year," he told her.

"Let's get back to Wilder Enterprises and the CD-ROM stuff."

"It involves storing information onto compact disks and then reading them on your computer. How about your own library with 450 of the world's greatest books on one disk?"

"Who would want to stare at a screen instead of reading a book in the comfort of their own easy chair?" she asked, mystified by the very idea.

"They have computers small enough to hold in the palm of your hand," Roy reminded her. "The twenty-first century is right around the corner, you know."

"Don't remind me," she muttered.

"So why the interest in Wilder Enterprises?"

"I just ran into Kane Wilder...."

"No kidding? He's considered to be a visionary in the computer technology of the future. A regular whiz kid."

"He's no kid," Susannah retorted, "although he does have a kid brother. Our own Charles the Intern."

"Which one is he?" Roy asked.

The lying, deceitful one, Susannah was tempted to reply. Instead she said, "The dark-haired one with the wire-rimmed glasses."

"Sounds like nerdiness runs in the family," Roy noted with a laugh.

Guess again, Susannah thought to herself. If there was a nerdy bone in Kane Wilder's body, she hadn't seen it. His dark business suit had a European cut that spoke of quiet elegance. Not a nerdy plastic penholder in sight. The only nonconforming element of his attire had been the tie he'd been wearing, as she only now recalled the tiny blue computer screens that had adorned the burgundy silk.

He might have been attractive, had it not been for the way he'd glared at her. Not the kind of man to make an apology easily. But apologize to her he would, because he'd made a mistake big-time when he'd crossed her. Talk about computer chips might make her tremble, but Kane Wilder she could handle!

Kane entered his hotel room and headed straight for the phone. His afternoon had been consumed with taking care of his company's business. Now it was time for family business.

Automatically punching in the numbers for his calling card, Kane reflected back on his meeting with Susannah Hall. It hadn't gone as well as he'd hoped. He hated surprises, and she'd certainly been one.

He'd expected something different, *someone* different—not a sweet-faced, sharp-tongued woman with a temper to match his. And big brown eyes that seemed to secretly laugh at him, effectively telling him that she thought he was an idiot.

Kane wasn't accustomed to being looked at that way. Most people considered him to be of above-average intelligence. *Way* above. He'd skipped ahead two years in grade school and another two in his college's accelerated program.

The bottom line was that Kane had been called "gifted" by his teachers and "good-looking" by the women in his life. He prided himself on not conforming to the nerdy stereotype so many of his cohorts were tagged with. He'd been called "a maverick" and "a loner" accustomed to being on his own.

But he wasn't entirely on his own. He never had been. He had Chuck. Their mother had died when Chuck was only four. Kane had been fourteen—ready, willing and able to take his brother under his wing to protect him from their abusive alcoholic father. The old man had finally drunk himself to death on the eve of Kane's eighteenth birthday. Kane held no fond memories of his father.

With help from Philip Durant, his counselor at the Massachusetts Institute of Technology, Kane had petitioned the court for legal custody of his then eight-year-old brother. Philip and his wife had become surrogate grandparents to Chuck and firm believers in Kane's determination to make a better life for himself and his brother.

Now Kane *had* that better life, but his brother didn't seem to appreciate it one bit. Kane wished Philip or his wife were still alive to advise him, but they'd both passed away in a car accident two years ago. Kane still missed them, especially at moments like this.

The sound of his sister-in-law's voice interrupted his thoughts.

"Hi, Ann," he said with deliberate cheerfulness. Despite his initial misgivings about the advisability of his brother marrying at the young age of nineteen, he'd decided that Ann was good for Chuck. She kept his feet on the ground. At least she always had in the past. She was a sweet girl and she deserved better than this, Kane noted savagely. But his voice reflected none of his inner feelings as he asked to speak to his brother.

"He's not here right now," Ann replied in an unsteady voice that was husky with tears.

"What happened?" Kane demanded gently, not wanting to set his sister-in-law off again. "Did you two have another argument?"

"Chuck doesn't really argue, you know that. He just quietly does whatever he wants."

Kane swore softly. "I've been too easy on him."

"Don't blame yourself," Ann said. "We both know there's only one person to blame. *Her.* Did you find her? Did you talk to her?"

Since this entire thing had begun, Ann had refused to use Susannah's given name. Kane had told Ann about his intention of confronting Susannah once he'd discovered she was attending the conference. Working out of Boston as he did, this was his first chance to meet Susannah. "I found her and I talked to her," he replied.

"What did she say?"

Kane was reluctant to tell Ann that Susannah Hall claimed she was innocent of any wrongdoing. Until Kane could talk to his brother himself, he decided not to be too specific about the details.

"Don't you worry, Ann," he reassured her. "I've got *everything* under control."

Susannah was running late. So what else was new? she asked herself as she dumped her briefcase on the bed and kicked off her high heels. She sighed in relief, rubbing her toes as she sat on the bed for a second to catch her breath.

Two heartbeats later, her second was up. She headed for the closet. She only had half an hour to get ready for the big party tonight.

It was a must-attend function and promised to be a spectacular spread. The organizers had rented one of Savannah's most impressive historical homes for the evening. Everything had been taken care of: from providing charter buses to take participants from their hotels to the historical district, right down to supplying rental costumes in the requested sizes.

Susannah's period costume had arrived while she was still at the convention center, so it was with some trepidation that she pulled back the opaque garment bag to reveal a lovely dress in deep red velvet. She couldn't believe the costume company had actually supplied her with the right color and size.

Finally, something was going right! Although she'd never admit it to a living soul, Kane's appearance as an avenging angel this afternoon had thrown her. So had his accusations.

After stripping off her business suit, she carefully tugged the dress over her head. She was relieved to see that it *did* fit. She wasn't relieved by the amount of cleavage it showed.

The dress, which zipped at the side so she was able to fasten it herself, had a long skirt, ending just above her ankles. After a long day on her feet, she wasn't about to cramp her feet into another pair of high heels for what would no doubt be more standing tonight, so she instead chose a pair of velvet flats.

Unfortunately, there wasn't time to do much with her hair. Savannah's springtime humidity had turned her dark waves into an uncontrollable mop. The best she could do was pin it up so she wouldn't get too hot.

The finishing touch to her outfit was an antique garnet necklace that was a favorite of hers. A matching pair of drop earrings and bracelet completed the set, which she'd inherited from her great-grandmother. Normally, Susannah didn't bring the set on a business trip, but the promise of the costume party tonight had been too good an opportunity to resist.

Glancing at her watch, she swore softly. She only had five minutes to get downstairs and catch the charter bus going to the party. Susannah grabbed her purse and was out in the hallway before realizing that she should have switched to a smaller bag.

Such was her life in a nutshell, Susannah noted as she impatiently jabbed at the elevator button. She was *almost* organized. Almost together. But inevitably there would be one thing that threw a wrench in the plan. Tonight that one thing was her purse.

She was the last one to board the bus, where everyone was dressed to the nines. Once they reached the historical house, guests had to show their invitations at the door in order to be allowed inside. It took Susannah five minutes to find the gilt-edged invitation in her bag—which still held the apple she'd picked up for lunch, along with the personal cassette player she'd listened to on the flight that morning, among other things.

Slinging her purse back over her shoulder, and almost decking the man behind her, Susannah followed the crowd into the front parlor. The place was packed. Rather than head for the buffet table laden with food, she chose to join a tour that was gathering at the foot of the stairs.

On her way there she bumped into someone, or more accurately her purse did. "Sorry," she said with a smile that evaporated as she recognized Kane Wilder. "What are you doing here?" she demanded.

"Looking for you," Kane replied. "I told you I wasn't done talking to you."

"Well, I'm done talking to you." With those words, she slipped past him and moved up the stairs with the rest of the tour group. To her dismay, Kane followed her.

"Only two people to a step, please," the tour guide requested when Kane joined her on the stairs. "We're trying to minimize the wear and tear on the structure."

Wanting to minimize the wear and tear on her own composure, Susannah strove to keep her attention focused on holding up the long skirt of her dress as she climbed the steps. It was better than thinking about Kane—who was directly behind her.

He'd looked incredibly dashing in his black formal wear, white tie and tails complete with a starched collar true to the Victorian period. She could feel his eyes on her and she wished she were ten pounds lighter. Maybe fifteen. The dress did nothing to hide her full figure.

Kane was enjoying the view of Susannah Hall's velvet-covered derriere. The stiff set of her bare shoulders radiated an ice-age chill. With her hair pinned up, he could see her pale nape as she leaned forward. For the first time since he'd arrived, he was glad he'd decided to attend this bash.

He'd been tempted to stay in his hotel room and wait for his brother's call, but past experience told him that Chuck wouldn't be back for some time yet. When his brother got in a snit, he tended to brood for hours. Kane would check in with him again when this party was over. Meanwhile, he planned on hounding Susannah until she relented and agreed to leave his brother alone.

At the moment, the tour guide was the only one talking. "The Whitaker house is a fine example of Federal architecture. In its heyday this house was at the center of Savannah society. At its low point, it was an apartment tenement in the 1930s and was almost torn down in the 1950s to build a parking lot when, thankfully, the Historical Preservation League saved it."

Susannah shuddered to think of this lovely home being demolished and paved over. Sensing Kane coming closer, she edged around the person ahead of her. Throughout the tour of the second floor she managed to weave her way in and out of the crowd, always staying one step ahead of him.

"As you can see," their guide continued, "the second floor houses the family's bedrooms, which have been decorated with period furnishings. On the wall along the stairway you'll see several family portraits, including that of Elsbeth Whitaker—who is said to have committed suicide on these very steps."

Susannah rubbed her hands over her bare arms as a chill settled over her. She couldn't see the painting due to the crowd of people still clustered in the hallway where she stood. Then the crowd parted and she saw a flash of the portrait—a white face and sad eyes. The image lingered even after she'd turned away.

"What's up on the third floor?" someone asked.

"It's a storage area that's presently under construction and being renovated. It's not open to the public," the guide replied. "Now, on our way back down, remember that only two people are allowed on a step at a time, so please come down the stairs slowly and in groups of two."

"We need to talk," Kane growled in her ear. "I'm not letting you off the hook until you promise to stay away from my brother."

"Go away!" she hissed, angrily pulling back from him. She needed to lose him and fast. She was feeling unsettled enough as it was, tonight. She wasn't in the mood for any more confrontations. But there was no place to hide. Unless... Her gaze was drawn upstairs. Maybe she could ditch Kane by sneaking upstairs and waiting a few minutes until the coast was clear.

While the tour guide's back was turned and she still had the protection of the crowd, Susannah did just that. She didn't take time to think about her actions. She just did it. It was almost as if she were compelled to do so.

Kane was about to go down when he saw her out of the corner of his eye. Susannah was going *up* the stairs. Muttering under his breath, he went after her, slipping past the tour guide. He wasn't going to let her get away from him that easily.

Instead of a storage room under construction as the tour guide had claimed, he saw a room that looked to be completely furnished although very dimly lit with a sort of flickering candlelight. He also saw Susannah, just over the threshold of that room.

Not wanting to get caught in a restricted area before he had a chance to talk to her, he whispered her name when he wanted to shout it.

Paying him no heed, Susannah moved forward, away from him and toward a bright blue light that was coming from a rocking chair in the far corner near the other entrance into the room.

Enchanted, Susannah forgot all about Kane. She was drawn forward, as if pulled by invisible forces. The nearer she got, the more the light shifted away from her toward the second doorway. Following it, for one instant she saw a face amid the ethereal blue light—it was the face of the woman in the portrait!

Kane was right behind Susannah as she reached out to touch the pool of light, but it disappeared as they stepped through the second doorway after it. Whatever it was they'd witnessed had vanished!

"Did you see that?" Susannah asked in a whisper. When he made no reply, she said, "You're not going to tell me that you didn't see it, are you?"

"I'm not telling you anything except to stay away from my brother," Kane replied curtly.

"You sound like a broken record," she informed him before hurrying back downstairs.

Kane let her go. She'd caused him enough aggravation for one day. He'd talk to her again tomorrow, get her promise to stay away from his brother then. God knew, he'd had an exhausting day with little to eat. As for that strange light they'd seen upstairs...it must have been a hologram, perhaps a future exhibit of some kind for the historical house.

The party was in full force now. The rooms were packed with people, all looking rather solemn. Glancing around, Kane didn't see anyone he knew. With a crowd this large, he wasn't surprised. After all, this was his first publishing convention. Normally he demonstrated his CD-ROM material at computer shows.

Heading straight for the food spread, he eyed the offerings with suspicion. Nothing looked good. And nothing looked substantial enough to stop the growling in his stomach. He remembered seeing a soda machine by the gift shop in the back of the house but when he headed that way, he couldn't find it. Or the gift shop. But then, the house was a maze of rooms. Crowded rooms.

Kane tugged at his stiff collar again. "Damned monkey suit," he muttered under his breath, sliding a finger beneath his collar and grimacing at the tightness of the fit. The place was getting unbearably hot. The air conditioner must not be working properly. That or the organizers were really sticking to historical accuracy for this party.

Either way, it was the last straw. Deciding that enough was enough, Kane opted to skip the rest of the party and go grab a cheeseburger and a huge cola with an extra order of fries. He was able to find the front door, although it took him a while to get there through the mad crush of people. He reached the front entrance the same time Susannah did.

"After you," he said with a mocking bow that almost cut off his circulation at his Adam's apple. The damn collar would be the death of him yet.

"I don't know about you, but I've had enough of this fancy-dress stuff," he announced as they stepped outside. "I'm heading for the closest fast-food joint and grabbing a thick cheeseburger with everything on it." And after that, Kane planned on calling his brother.

Moving forward, he bumped into Susannah as she halted on the steps in front of him.

"Something's not right," Susannah murmured. Looking around, she searched for the cause of her uneasiness. She'd always been a great believer in trusting her instincts. Some people called it jumping to conclusions. Her grandmother claimed it was a touch of second sight. Whatever you called it, Susannah trusted the feeling.

The house faced a small park, one of many in this part of the city. The street had been lined with parked cars when they'd arrived. Now there were none. No cars anywhere— none parked, moving, nothing. "The cars are gone," she noted aloud.

Kane looked around. "What cars? I came by bus."

"There were cars parked all along the park across the street. Now they're gone."

"Probably only allowed to park there during the day," he logically explained.

She shook her head. "Something just doesn't feel right. There isn't any traffic, either."

"You've got an overactive imagination, do you know that?"

To which she replied, "I didn't imagine that blue light upstairs. The one on the third floor. Surely you saw it, too?"

Kane didn't answer as a couple walked by on the sidewalk. They were wearing costumes similar to those worn at the party and he was preparing to move aside to let them enter the house—when they walked past and entered a home a few doors down.

Susannah saw the couple, too, and the house they entered: a building she could have sworn was boarded up and empty when they'd arrived earlier that evening. "I'm telling you, I've got a bad feeling about this," she murmured.

# Two
***

"So you've got a bad feeling," Kane retorted. "Probably caused by that crab dip at the party."

"Very funny. Don't tell me you don't feel it, too."

"I don't eat crab dip."

"I'm serious. Didn't you see that couple walk into that house?" she demanded.

"Sure, I did." Kane shrugged. "So what?"

"They were dressed—"

"In the same kind of stupid clothes we are," he interrupted her. "Which means that there must be several houses being used for costume parties tonight. The publishing convention is huge. There must be plenty of these fancy shindigs being put on."

"Perhaps, but I could have sworn that that building was boarded up when we got here earlier this evening. And how do you explain that blue light, that specter thing we saw up on the third floor?"

"Holograms," Kane instantly replied. "It's being done

all the time. Haven't you ever been to Disney World?''

Susannah didn't buy his explanation for one minute. "I sincerely doubt that a historical house like this would be able to invest the money required for that kind of special effects— Wait a second! Look at the lights—''

"I told you it was a hologram," he interrupted her again.

"I mean the streetlights," she continued in a shaken voice. "They're not electric."

"Of course, they're not. This is a historic district."

Looking around, Susannah murmured, "There are no telephone lines, either."

"They're mostly underground these days."

"Not everywhere. I'm telling you, there were telephone lines here when we arrived tonight. I distinctly remember them ruining the view."

Just then, a horse and buggy went by.

Anticipating what she was going to say, Kane explained, "For the tourists."

Another buggy went by, and then several men on horseback. Still no sign of a car, or truck or bus. Seeing Susannah's expression, he said, "Okay, I admit this is starting to look a little strange. They're certainly taking this period thing to extremes. Reminds me of Williamsburg. They take this re-creation thing to extremes there, too."

"But we're not in a historic village here. We're in the middle of downtown Savannah."

"Which has a fast-food place right around the corner and a burger with my name on it," Kane declared with a sense of anticipation.

"I'll join you," Susannah hurriedly said.

"I didn't ask you to join me."

"It's still a free country," she defensively countered, determined to keep him by her side—which only went to show how uneasy she was feeling. Normally, Kane Wilder would be the last man she'd want to spend any additional time with. But then, nothing about their surroundings felt *normal*. Even the street pavement seemed different.

No more words were spoken as they briskly walked the short distance, Susannah trying to keep up despite the hindrance of her long skirt. Concentrating on holding up her hem in order not to have it drag on the ground, she almost rammed into Kane, who was standing frozen in the middle of the sidewalk. The man was solidly built, she hazily noted, especially for someone who was said to be a computer whiz kid. But then, as she'd told Roy from Marketing, Kane Wilder was no kid. He was too good-looking for his own good and he was wearing an all-too-familiar frown on his face. "It was right here," he muttered, "and now it's gone." Turning to glare at her, he demanded, "What is this?"

"I don't know," she replied, trying not to panic. "I told you I had a bad feeling about this."

"I must have gotten my directions turned around," Kane muttered. "Maybe the burger place was this way." Pivoting on his heel, he turned right and headed down the street only to find that there was nothing but houses in what should have been a commercial business area.

Frowning, Kane gave Susannah a look that clearly stated he held her responsible for this situation. "What's going on here? Did you slip something into my drink? Either that or the punch I drank was a hell of a lot stronger than I thought," he noted in an undertone as yet another buggy passed them by. "I must be either drunk or hallucinating."

"*I* had nothing to drink at the party at all. And it's highly unlikely we'd both be having the same hallucination," Susannah observed, trying to be logical about things. It was the only way she could cope with their present circumstances—to take the situation bit by bit. Not to look at the large picture. Not yet.

"Then I must be dreaming," Kane muttered. "That or I'm dead."

"How do you figure that?" she demanded, chilled by his comment.

But he wasn't listening to her anymore. "There's only one way to find out."

To her amazement he marched off, straight toward—

"Watch out!" Susannah shouted.

Kane ignored her warning . . . and walked smack into one of the metal streetlamp posts.

Picking up her skirts, Susannah rushed to his side as he stood swaying slightly.

"That was a stupid thing to do!" she told him. "What were you thinking of?"

"Hypothesis."

She looked at him as if he'd scrambled his brain.

"I figured if I was dreaming, walking into the lamppost would wake me up," Kane said, his voice brusque. "And if I was dead—"

"We're not dead and we're not dreaming," she interrupted him.

"Fine, Einstein, then what *are* we doing?"

"I'm not positive," she noted in a soft voice, as if speaking too loudly might cause them even further trouble. "But I think Einstein had a theory about this—the relativity of time."

"Meaning what?"

"Meaning that something happened. We're clearly not in the 1990s, anymore," she stated, trying to sound as if this were a situation she'd run into before. The truth was that her instincts were on red alert. And, as her grandmother had always told her, Susannah had always had *excellent* instincts. She and Kane weren't dead. They weren't hallucinating. She felt sure of that. Which left precious few alternatives.

Susannah paused, only now noticing a paper pasted to the lamppost Kane had walked into. Peering closer, she gasped as she read the date on the handbill advertising a circus coming to town. Her instincts had been right. "Look at this handbill!"

"Unless it's got directions to the nearest hamburger I'm not interested," Kane muttered, rubbing the goose egg quickly rising on his forehead.

Someone was approaching them on the sidewalk. A man wearing a hat, and using a cane. A bushy muttonchop beard covered a great deal of his face. His clothing was like something from a movie set—one of those period pieces the film critics liked so much.

*Was the man able to see them?* Susannah wondered. *Hear them?* There was only one way to find out. "Excuse me, sir," she hesitantly asked. "Could you tell me the time, please?"

The gentleman gave her a leery look, which meant he could see her and hear her, as well. Thank heavens! Relieved that at least she and Kane weren't invisible, Susannah released the breath she hadn't even realized she'd been holding.

Pulling his watch from his fob pocket, the man said, "The time is quarter past nine."

"Thank you." She could tell he was impatient to move on, so she went right to the heart of the matter. "And the year is...?"

At her question, the gentleman's leery look now turned downright suspicious. "What kind of foolish prank is this? The year is 1884, of course."

Susannah went cold all over. The year he'd just given her matched that on the circus handbill. She'd had her suspicions...but even so, hearing them confirmed—hearing the man say that it was 1884—left her feeling as if a rug had been yanked out from under her.

Eyeing Kane, who was still a bit unsteady on his legs, the bewhiskered gentleman muttered something about the downfall of civilization being caused by an overindulgence in alcohol before hurrying on his way.

It took her a moment before she could speak. "Did you hear that?" she whispered to Kane.

"Yeah, he thought I was drunk," Kane replied irritably.

"The part before that. About the year being...1884."

Kane nodded, grimacing as he did so. His head was hurting like hell. "I heard what he said. The old guy clearly isn't playing with a full deck. Surely you're not buying what he said, are you?"

"It would certainly explain a lot."

"Oh yeah, right," Kane noted mockingly.

"What if we have somehow traveled back in time?"

"It's too ridiculous to even consider. Come on." Grabbing her hand, Kane led her toward a larger thoroughfare with more foot traffic. "I'll prove it to you."

Everyone was dressed in period clothing suitable for the late 1800s. The crowd was mostly male. The gaslight from the streetlamps lacked the harshness of the piercing orange lights used in so many cities these days. All of Susannah's senses were bombarded with proof of the time—the strong smell of horse manure mixed with human perspiration, the dull *clip-clop* sound of horses maneuvering buggies down the busy thoroughfare. The street itself wasn't asphalt or blacktop but appeared to be softer, perhaps dirt or sand. Even the sidewalk beneath her feet was different—constructed of red bricks.

Everyone was wearing hats. Except Kane and her. While Susannah had been taking stock of the people, she realized Kane was approaching everyone walking by, asking them what year it was.

Recognizing the disapproving and suspicious looks being cast their way, Susannah tugged on her hand—the one Kane was holding in a cast-iron grip—bringing his attention back to her. "What are you going to do, keep asking until you hear an answer you like, or until they call the police?" she demanded in an undertone.

"Since when has asking a simple question been illegal?" Kane countered.

"Stop this," she hissed, yanking her hand free of his grasp. "You're embarrassing me."

"We may have fallen through a time hole and you're worried about being embarrassed?" he asked in disbelief.

Pulling him around the corner and out of the flow of foot traffic, she said, "I'm worried about being put in an asylum, the way you're behaving! Trust me, they don't treat people very nicely in Bellevue, or the local equivalent, in this day and age. So try not to make a spectacle of yourself, okay? We don't want to draw attention to ourselves." Tucking her hand in his arm, she led him back the way they'd come, deliberately walking at a slow and leisurely pace. Besides, with the long skirt of her heavy velvet dress, she could only travel at two speeds—slow and slower.

"This is all your fault," Kane muttered, his head still throbbing. As they passed the infamous lamppost, he glared at it, before turning to glare at her. "Something must have happened when we stepped in that damn blue light. I told you not to go into that room!"

"No one held a gun to your head and made you come after me," she retorted. "Listen, it's useless to toss around accusations at this point. We have to go back into that room."

He headed for the brick front steps of the house where they'd seen the blue light upstairs. "Fine. The sooner the better."

"Wait a second. How are we going to get back inside?"

"By opening the door." He did so before she could protest.

A servant hurried across the hall to greet them. "May I help you, sir?"

"We left something here earlier," Kane explained. "Nothing to worry about. We'll only be a minute."

Luckily, another servant carrying a full tray of food required the first servant's assistance in the crowded front parlor, thereby momentarily giving Kane and Susannah the free access to the stairway they required.

As Susannah quietly passed the doorway leading to the crowded parlor, she only now realized that while the party was still going on, the mood was definitely more somber than festive. Then her attention was focused on catching up with Kane, who was already halfway up the staircase.

Once they were safely on the third floor, she turned to him and said in dismay, "There's no blue light here anymore!"

"Don't panic. Try and remember exactly what we did. Maybe if we reenact everything exactly, we'll end up back where we started, in our own time."

Susannah nodded. It sounded as logical a suggestion as any she could come up with. "I got to the top of the staircase here and saw the blue light coming from the room. Then I moved from the landing over to this doorway. It was almost as if I was being drawn forward. There was this same flickering candlelight, but the brightest light—that strange blue light that isn't here anymore—was coming from the rocking chair over there by the second door. I reached out to touch it, but it disappeared as I stepped through this second doorway." As she softly spoke the words, she went through the motions she was describing. Then she stepped over the threshold, with Kane right on her heels, almost tripping on the hem of her red velvet dress.

"Did it work?" he demanded. "Are we back in our own time now?"

Peering out the third-story window, Susannah said, "I don't think so. Hey, did you know that there's a mirror up here aimed at the front porch? From the angle it's set at, you can see who's at the door."

"Would you stop gushing over the furnishings," Kane exclaimed irritably, "and do something useful instead."

"I never gush," Susannah haughtily informed him before another thought struck her. "I remember something else. For one second, I'm sure I saw a face in that strange blue light. The face of that woman in the portrait. Elsbeth."

"Look, I'm willing to acknowledge the possibility of time travel here, but I draw the line at ghosts," Kane stated emphatically.

*Help!*

Susannah's eyes widened. "Did you hear that?" she whispered.

"Hear what?"

*Help me!*

Susannah's breath caught, at both the painful urgency of the woman's voice and the realization that she was hearing it inside her head. Could it be... Elsbeth? Was she communicating with her?

*Did you bring us here?* It was more a thought on Susannah's part rather than a deliberate attempt to talk to the now-invisible ghost. She could see no sign of Elsbeth's presence, but she did feel something.... She shivered and ran her hands up her bare forearms.

*Are you there?* Susannah felt the silent confirmation rather than heard it.

*Did you bring us here?*

Again the silent confirmation.

*But why?*

This time Susannah heard the whispery reply in her mind: *To help me.*

"Help you how?" Susannah asked aloud.

It was as if her spoken words temporarily cut off the silent bond between herself and Elsbeth, if that's what it was, for there was no longer any reply. And Susannah's own sixth sense told her that she was temporarily on her own here, aside from an irritated-looking Kane.

"I said I could use some help," Kane told her.

Was that what she'd heard? Kane asking for her help? Had she just imagined the ghostly presence communicating with her?

"Would you stop going all mistily sentimental on me and help me out, here?" Seeing her hesitation, Kane quickly added, "Do you want to be stuck in the past forever? Women don't even have the vote yet."

Sighing, Susannah acknowledged that he did have a good point. Their first priority had to be finding a way home. The idea of helping out a ghost did sound a little farfetched. Not that the concept of jumping a century in the blink of an eye was an everyday occurrence, either. "What do you want me to do?"

Stepping back inside the room, Kane said, "Try pushing on the walls."

She did so, while asking, "What are we looking for?"

"I don't know. Anything unusual. A time portal, maybe."

"Sounds like something out of a science-fiction novel," she noted with a nervous laugh. This entire situation was too bizarre for words. So much of it felt dreamlike, yet there was a hard-edged reality to it that dispelled any hope she had that she was dreaming.

Between them, they pushed on every square inch of wall space in the relatively small room. Nothing happened. After nearly an hour had passed, Susannah became more and more discouraged. As a last resort, she closed her eyes, clicked her heels together three times and whispered, "There's no place like home, there's no place like home, there's no place like home."

Upon opening her eyes, the first thing she saw was the derisive expression on Kane's face. "Stop looking at me that way! It worked for Dorothy," she said defensively.

"Well, it didn't work for us," he noted.

His glance lowered to the low neckline of her dress, which Susannah was disconcerted to discover he appeared to be studying with more than casual interest. Suddenly the words he'd thrown at her in the convention center that afternoon came back to her. A Mata Hari who played bedroom games with younger, married men—wasn't that what he'd said? Or something to that effect. With that in mind, Susannah didn't like the way he was eyeing her one bit.

She was tempted to put a hand up to shield her exposed skin from his hot gaze. But that would be admitting that he bothered her, and she wasn't about to give him that advantage over her. So she threw back her shoulders instead and narrowed her eyes, as if daring him to make a comment. When he did, it was far from what she expected.

"Where did you get that necklace you're wearing?" he demanded curtly.

Now her hand did fly up, to cover her necklace rather than her skin. "Why do you want to know?" she countered distrustfully.

"Because the woman in the portrait along the stairs is wearing one identical to it."

"Elsbeth?" Stepping into the hallway and down a few steps, Susannah studied the portrait of Elsbeth Whitaker. Kane had blocked her view when she'd hurried upstairs an hour before. Now she could see the black bunting draped around the portrait. That hadn't been there when the tour guide had talked about the painting in their own century. Susannah was familiar enough with Victorian tradition to know that such bunting was only used on a portrait to indicate the subject's death. Her heart fell.

"She's died already. We're too late to save her," she murmured.

"Save her?" Kane repeated. "Listen, I may not know much about time travel, but even *I* know that you're not supposed to mess with things like life and death. What if this woman later had children who went on to become mass murderers or something?"

"Then why did she bring us here?"

"Who said she did?"

"I do. I can feel it here." She pressed her palm against her heart. She'd also gotten confirmation from Elsbeth, but she didn't think this was the best time to confess she'd communicated with a ghost. For she now felt sure that that's what she'd done—communicated with Elsbeth. She *hadn't* imagined it.

"Is the woman some kind of relative of yours?" Kane demanded.

Susannah shook her head. "I don't have any relatives in Savannah."

"How can you be sure?" he argued.

"Because I recently did a family history—a family tree, if you will—for my parents' anniversary and I traced our ancestry back to the 1700s. Elsbeth Whitaker's name didn't show up, I'm sure of it."

"Then how do you explain the necklace? It's exactly the same as yours. Were a lot of them made during that time?"

Again, Susannah shook her head. "This one was specially made to order for my great-grandmother." Looking into the sad eyes of the woman in the portrait, she felt a strong sense of kinship. Her instincts told her that her necklace, the one that so exactly matched the one Elsbeth was wearing, was some kind of tie.

She scrambled to put the pieces together. Had her great-grandmother gotten the necklace from Elsbeth somehow? Perhaps the two women had known each other. Whatever the case might have been, Susannah only knew that she was here for a reason. All she had to do was figure out what that reason was. She didn't realize she'd spoken her words aloud until Kane replied.

"And how do you plan on doing that?" he demanded.

"By getting more information about Elsbeth Whitaker."

"How? By asking the people downstairs about her suicide?"

"Of course not. Nothing that crass. That's more your style than mine."

"Oh, right," he retorted. "Like you're the soul of discretion. I think not."

"Think whatever you please," she countered.

He groaned. "God, you're even starting to sound like this time period."

"I happen to have edited a book or two on this era, luckily for you."

"Oh, yeah, I'm certainly counting my blessings about now," Kane returned sarcastically.

"Just keep quiet and listen. You might learn a thing or two."

"From you?"

"From the people at the party downstairs. The faster we can figure out what's going on here, the faster we can get back to our own time period," she reminded him.

Having attended more publishing cocktail parties than she cared to, Susannah had the moves down pat—just stand around the edge of the room, with eyes downcast, and tune in to the conversations going on all around. It was her way of surviving the stifling artificiality of the business functions she was required to attend. By nature she was more a romantic dreamer than a go-getting extrovert.

To her right, two bearded men—one with a black beard, the other with a red one—were talking about some book they'd recently purchased. It took Susannah a moment to realize they were talking about none other than Mark Twain's *The Prince and the Pauper.*

To her left, two women were speaking about the joys of matrimony. "It has ever been my opinion that a woman must learn to relinquish self and live for another in order for her to have a truly happy marriage."

"Verily so. Perhaps that's why Elsbeth wasn't happy in her marital situation. But to have things end so tragically. . . ." The words were a mere whisper now, and Susannah had to strain to hear them. "The scandal is unimaginable. Such things simply don't happen in our circles."

The other woman nodded. "I wasn't sure about attending tonight's function, but we'd accepted months ago. My husband said that tonight was primarily a business gathering and therefore wouldn't be inappropriate, considering the circumstances. My etiquette manual said nothing about an instance such as this, so I was left to depend upon my husband's judgment in this matter."

"As you should in all things."

Susannah's feminist blood was boiling, but there was no time for that now. She was getting curious looks from several of those attending the gathering. Looking at the other women present and comparing her dress to theirs, she realized that her outfit was off by a couple decades or more. And no one had a purse the size of hers. They all had dainty little reticules dangling from their wrists, while her shoulder bag felt like it was the size of New Jersey. The bottom line was that she was attracting attention, and she certainly didn't want to do that.

Nodding at Kane, who was a short distance away, she shot her gaze toward the door in a hopefully discreet indication that it was time to make a fast exit. To her relief, Kane got her silent message and a minute later they were outside once again.

"So what did you find out?" Kane demanded.

"That the women of this era were downtrodden and brainwashed," Susannah tartly replied.

"Wonderful. That's extremely helpful."

"Okay, so what did *you* find out?"

"That they're still talking about the first baseball game held under electric lights in June of last year. In Fort Wayne, Indiana, of all places. Oh, and that a horse named Buchanan won the tenth annual Kentucky Derby a few days ago."

"That's it?"

"No. I also found out these people dislike Republicans and they don't approve of the way the government is being run. I didn't recognize any of the names they mentioned. Even though it's been twenty years since the Civil War ended, apparently they still have a few lingering carpetbaggers from up north to contend with."

"We're lucky we didn't land in the middle of the war," Susannah noted.

They were walking as they talked. The night was still and the air thick with humidity. Susannah could feel her hair going berserk, corkscrew curls forming in rebellion against being unnaturally restricted. Sure enough, a hairpin slid down and dangled over her left ear while several strands of her hair spiraled in uncontrollable wildness. Muttering under her breath, she jabbed the hairpin back in place.

"Are you listening to me?" Kane demanded impatiently.

"Not really," she readily admitted. "And you can stop glaring at me. You've done it so often in the past twelve hours that I've become immune to it."

To her amazement, he actually smiled at her—a slow, riverboat gambler's smile that made his blue eyes gleam in the gaslit evening. He looked dashing. She remembered thinking so when she'd first seen him at the party earlier.

Then she'd seen that fateful blue light, a lighter blue than his eyes, she absently noted. His smile really did have a devilish edge to it. She hadn't expected that. Nor the breathless feeling it caused.

Of course, after zipping back 111 years in a single step, who wouldn't be breathless? It had nothing to do with his smile, she silently defended herself. Or his incredibly blue eyes.

"Wha-at—" She had to pause to clear her voice. "What are you looking at?"

"At you. You've got a hairpin hanging over your eyebrow."

"Where?" She automatically reached up.

"No. It's over here." He brushed her left temple with his index finger. The merest of touches and yet it branded her with unexpected intensity.

"Yes, well..." She cleared her throat again. "We need to decide what to do next."

"That answer is obvious. The first thing we have to do is get some nineteenth-century money," Kane stated.

"And how do you propose we do that?"

By this time they'd reached another area of fairly heavy foot traffic. As before, Susannah only saw one other woman in the area. She was standing in front of what appeared to be a tavern of some kind. While Susannah was no expert in nineteenth-century fashion, she sincerely doubted that the amount of bare leg and petticoat the blowsy blonde was showing was appropriate for anything other than a lady of the night.

Seeing Kane, the other woman's eyes lit up. With dollar signs, no doubt, Susannah cynically reflected.

Kane noticed the woman, too, which aggravated Susannah for some reason. "What are you going to do?" Susannah addressed her mocking question to Kane. "Ask her what year it is?"

The woman apparently overheard them. "What year do you want it to be?" she asked Kane while moving closer to walk her fingers up his shirt buttons. "I can do whatever you want. Cost you only two bits."

"Such a bargain," Susannah noted caustically. "Cheap at half the price."

"Watch who you're callin' cheap!" the woman loudly exclaimed.

A man with a white apron tied around his waist came outside to investigate. "Now, Polly, you know better than to accost the customers. You know how the boss feels about that. He's trying to run a proper place now."

"Aw, Jed . . ." The woman's voice turned wheedling.

Jed ignored her. "Do come on in, sir. And please excuse Polly's boldness. Polly, take your friend—" the man pointed at Susannah "—and move along."

Susannah couldn't believe her ears. In 1995 Kane called her a Mata Hari, and here in 1884 she was being mistaken for a streetwalker! Clearly she was suffering from an image problem. Was it her perfume? she wondered with wry amusement. Her walk?

Don't go off the deep end on me now, she lectured herself, snapping out of her momentary reverie to curtly say, "I am no friend of Polly's."

"That's right," Kane confirmed. "She's with me."

"Begging your pardon, sir. I didn't mean no disrespect. It's just that we don't get many decent women in here."

"Well, you're about to get one now," Susannah haughtily informed him, striding through the doorway, only to stop in her tracks at the force of fifty lascivious eyes turned to focus on her.

"What happened to keeping a low profile?" Kane dryly inquired in her ear.

She told herself her shiver was caused by the fifty-or-so eyes still trained on her. But the truth was it was caused by the feel of Kane's warm breath tickling her ear. Since she'd always been ticklish that way, it was no big deal. Or so she told herself.

Getting out of this bar was a big deal, though. And something she planned on doing immediately.

But Kane had other ideas. Sensing she was about to bolt, he circled her arm with his fingers. "You're not going anywhere. I told you that we need money."

She stared at him in disbelief. "Well, I'm not about to earn it the way Polly out there does!"

For one split second his gaze slid down her body as if he were mentally undressing her. It was what the twenty-five other men in the room had done when she'd first walked in. But where their looks had turned her stomach, Kane's heated look curled her toes. And the feel of his fingers on the sensitive skin just above her elbow was creating more-than-justifiable havoc.

"Stop jumping to conclusions," he reprimanded her, his cool voice decidedly at odds with the intimate look he'd just given her. "Stay here a minute."

Without further ado he released her in order to stroll over to the bar where he began speaking to the bartender—Jed, the streetwalker had called him. Susannah stood nearby, close enough to Kane that the other men in the room wouldn't get any ideas about approaching her themselves, but too far away for her to hear what Kane and Jed were quietly discussing. While waiting, she fanned herself with her right hand. It was incredibly warm in the tavern. Downright stifling, in fact.

Remembering she had a fold-up fan in her purse, a convention giveaway, she dug inside the large bag hanging from her shoulder until she found what she was looking for. As she did so, she was struck by culture shock. When she'd gotten the free fan that morning, the year had been 1995 and she'd been a woman confident of her agenda.

Now she wasn't confident about much of anything; but one thing was sure—that old saying about you not missing something until it was gone was right on the money. Now that the conveniences of modern life were gone, Susannah missed them more than she could say. Air-conditioning topped the list. Air freshener and deodorant were right up there, too, she decided with a dainty sniff. The room could use the former and the men in it, the latter.

A few minutes later, Kane returned to her side. "Are we leaving now?" she asked hopefully.

"No. We're going to play some poker. Or more precisely, I'm going to play poker. You're going to stand nearby and keep quiet."

"Surely you jest," she retorted.

"Not at all."

"And how do you plan on playing poker with no money?"

"I suppose I could try and use you as the stakes," he responded teasingly.

She narrowed her eyes at him. "Try and die."

"Somehow I figured you'd say that. So we'll use your jewelry instead."

"What's with this 'we' business? And you're not getting your grubby hands on my jewels."

He raised an eyebrow at her, which gave him a devilish look that went well with his dark tux and tails.

"You know what I mean," she muttered.

"You have a brighter idea?"

"There must be another way. A more reliable way than gambling."

"If there is, we don't have time to find out," Kane said. "Jed tells me there's a game just beginning in the back room. You're welcome to wait outside with Polly, if you'd rather."

She gave him a look that would have withered a rattlesnake before coolly informing him, "I'd rather have an iced cappuccino in front of an air conditioner set on High, but that doesn't appear to be an option at the moment."

"You've got that right. You'll just have to make do with me."

The man was laughing at her, damn him! She was prepared to give him a tongue-lashing—to use the vernacular of the time—when he put his arm around her, as if to solicitously lead her through the crowd in the tavern to the back room and the poker game. As he did so, he whispered a warning in her ear. "Don't cause a scene here. Remember Bellevue."

Bellevue? He had that right! She belonged in a mental institution for agreeing to this harebrained plan of his. Unfortunately she couldn't come up with an alternative moneymaking scheme of her own at the moment.

So she kept quiet as Kane used the two rings she always wore—one a wide gold antique filigreed band she wore on her left hand, the other a half-carat channel-set diamond ring her parents had given her for her twenty-first birthday—as an opening stake into the game. Wryly wondering if her insurance policy covered losing her jewelry in a poker game held in 1884, Susannah was all too aware of the interested looks she was getting from the men in the smoky back room. Again, she was the only woman present.

The blue haze of cigar smoke was enough to make her stomach turn. Her queasiness was increased by the speed with which Kane began losing. Next he demanded her bracelet.

She immediately protested. "This was my—"

"Favorite bracelet. I know," Kane said in a curt voice. "I'll buy you another one."

Despite the fact that he was losing, something about his confidence had her handing over her garnet-and-gold bracelet. And then her matching earrings. But she'd refused to take off her great-grandmother's necklace. She absolutely drew the line there!

She watched with concern as the stack of coins Kane had been given dwindled to one. Kane had warned her not to say anything, but he was crazy if he thought she was going to stand here and watch him go into hock.

As if sensing her thoughts, he sent her a warning look before drawling, "Gentlemen, I appear to have a problem with dwindling resources."

"Too bad," a cigar-smoking man named J. P. Bellows said after spewing a series of perfect smoke rings. He was the most talkative of the bunch. "Appears I've won, then."

"Not so fast," Kane replied. "There's still my wife's necklace."

*Wife?* Susannah doubted her hearing. Her ears were starting to ring from exhaustion. She'd gotten up at four that morning to catch a flight from New York to Savannah and had arrived at the convention center a little before nine, spent the day on her feet with little to eat—not to mention time traveling 111 years. A person was bound to get a little jet-lagged under those circumstances.

Which no doubt explained why she thought she'd heard Kane describe her as his wife. Not that she was going to argue the point now. She'd seen the heated looks the Southern so-called gentlemen had been sending her way and she had a feeling their thoughts were as blue as the air. She had no intention of becoming the center of their unwanted attention. Kane was the lesser of two evils. For the moment, at least.

While she'd been momentarily distracted by her thoughts, Kane had finalized the arrangements for using her necklace as collateral for his latest bet. And, to her horror, he bet the entire amount on the cards he was holding.

"You're going to need more than a garnet necklace to call my bet," J.P. told Kane.

The room was suddenly still. Into the silence fell a sudden beep-beep.

"What was that?" J.P. demanded.

"My watch," Kane replied.

"I never heard a watch make that sound before."

"It's a very unusual watch."

"Let's see it, then."

Kane held out his wrist and showed them his watch, with its LCD digital display and numerous function buttons.

"That's no watch," J.P. scoffed. "Where's the face?"

"Doesn't need one. See, the time is displayed in numbers."

"Toss in that strange watch of yours and you've got a deal," J.P. declared.

"Done."

Susannah wished she knew enough about poker to know if his hand was good or not. The expression on his face gave nothing away. The dismay on hers no doubt encouraged the other men around the table.

Susannah clung to her necklace, which Kane had been wise enough not to try to remove from around her neck. Closing her eyes, she sent up a prayer.

Moments later she heard the collective groans from the other men at the table. Was that good or bad?

Her eyes flew open to see Kane raking a large pile of coins and paper money in his direction. "Did we win?"

"We won," he confirmed.

A wave of wild relief overtook her common sense. "Yes!" She let out a triumphant *whoop* worthy of a football fan while making an elated victorious gesture, fisting one hand and rocking back on one foot.

Seeing the openmouthed, wide-eyed stares of the men around the table, Kane knew he had to act fast. "My wife is prone to fits," he quickly stated. "There's only one cure."

"Fits?" she exclaimed in protest. The next thing she knew, he'd taken her in his arms and was kissing her. Totally caught off guard, Susannah didn't know what to do. She'd never expected such behavior from Kane. And who could have known he'd kiss like this—devilishly seductive, swooping down to capture her parted lips with utter confidence.

The heat, she told herself desperately. It was the heat. And he was generating plenty of it! Her lips quivered beneath his as he continued kissing her for another heart-stopping moment. She'd never been kissed this way in her entire life—as if she were Eve in the Garden of Eden. The passion was direct and all-consuming. Temptation. His kiss represented it. Promised it.

Desire shot through her system, rendering her speechless, even after he let her go. She blinked up at him, and saw in his eyes a flash of the same startled amazement she was feeling. That had been no ordinary kiss he'd just given her. It had been as sudden and intense as a bolt of lightning, coming out of nowhere and zapping her.

Okay, so traveling through time had rattled her. Shaken her to the soles of her feet, if the truth be known. That was understandable. Being rattled and shaken by his kiss wasn't. And it wasn't acceptable.

Unless it was just that the thrill of victory had momentarily left her senseless? Yes, that must have been it. She'd been that relieved that he'd won the poker game that she'd had a temporary bout of insanity. It was as good an explanation as any. It was less disturbing than the reality of being attracted to Kane Wilder.

She watched in silence as Kane gathered up his winnings. "Thank you, gentlemen," he told his fellow poker players. "It's been a very pleasurable experience." He shot a fiery look at Susannah as he said that.

"Wait, sir," J.P. protested. "You must give us the chance to recoup our losses."

"Another time, perhaps," Kane replied. "I must see to my wife's health. Could one of you recommend a respectable boardinghouse nearby?"

"There's one two blocks away," J.P. said. "Turn right once you get outside. You can't miss it."

"Thank you." With a nod, he returned Susannah's jewelry to her before taking her arm and gallantly escorting her out of the tavern.

Once outside, she gratefully inhaled the fresh air. Turning to face him, she said, "Fits? I'm prone to fits?"

"I had to tell them something."

"You didn't have to kiss me!"

"Yes, I did. They were getting suspicious. I had to distract them."

"Yes, well..." She floundered, the truth being he'd distracted *her* and how! "You're just lucky things worked out as well as they did."

"Luck had nothing to do with it," he replied, stashing the remainder of the nineteenth-century money in his inside coat pocket before taking her arm and setting off at a brisk pace.

"Are you saying you cheated?" Susannah demanded, struggling to keep up.

"Of course not."

"Then what did you mean?"

"That I'm an experienced poker player."

"Sure, you are. And that was why you were losing?"

"Exactly. I was baiting the hook and they snapped." Seeing her look of disbelief, he added, "Look, I've had a lot of experience testing software and one of the programs I designed a number of years back turned out to be the best-selling poker program on the market today. So trust me when I say that I knew what I was doing back there, okay?"

"No, it's not okay!" Susannah couldn't help herself. She socked him on the arm.

"Ow! What was that for?"

"For scaring me to death and not warning me what you were up to ahead of time!"

"And have you spill the beans by the look on your face? No way. Instead everything worked out just as I'd planned. You looked panic-stricken and that certainly helped our cause."

She couldn't help wondering if kissing her had been part of his master plan. Somehow she rather doubted it. He'd seemed as stunned as she was by the desire that had flared between them.

Rather than dwell on his kiss, she quickly latched on to another subject. "Wait a second. Why are we going this way? The man at the table told us that the boardinghouse was two blocks the *other* way."

"I checked with Jed, the bartender, ahead of time. That boardinghouse is a dump. But don't worry about a thing. I've got another place in mind. It's only about a fifteen-minute walk from here."

Five minutes of that time was spent trying to catch her breath at the fast pace he was setting. Her rented velvet dress felt as if it weighed a hundred pounds. "If you'd already spoken to Jed, then why did you ask those men about a boardinghouse?"

"Because I wanted them to think that's where we'd be staying in case one of them got the bright idea of trying to recover their money by stealing it back."

"Suspicious, aren't you?"

"I prefer cautious," he replied.

Susannah was both cautious and suspicious when she discovered, ten minutes later, the next surprise Kane had up his sleeve.

"I've already rented us a room," he declared.

# Three

―――――

"*A* room. As in one?" Susannah repeated in disbelief, her hand on his arm pulling Kane to a halt beside her. After having had him literally kiss her senseless a few minutes ago, she knew darn well that sharing a room with him would be too... tempting. Too dangerous to her peace of mind, she immediately corrected herself. "We'll need *two* rooms."

"I agree. We need two rooms."

"Good."

"Unfortunately we only have enough money to rent one room, which means—"

"That you're out of your mind if you think I'm going to share a room with you!"

"Believe me, I've already doubted my sanity more times than I can count this evening," Kane dryly countered. "But the fact remains that we only have enough money to rent one room."

"Allow me to remind you that my jewelry paid for this room."

"Correction. Your jewelry provided the initial *stakes*. My talent at playing poker quadrupled that stake. And don't forget the importance my watch played. Ah, here we are." He stood in front of a large three-story brick house. "Now try to remember that you're my wife and wives were quiet in these days."

"A typical male fantasy," she promptly retorted. "There have always been plenty of strong women, regardless of the century."

"And it's just my luck to get stuck with one of the stubbornest," Kane muttered. "We don't want to stand out, remember?"

"We're checking into a boardinghouse without any luggage," she mockingly reminded him. "Don't you think that's bound to raise a few eyebrows?"

"Just stay quiet and follow my lead," Kane said as he hurried her up the front steps to the stoop, where he paused to frown at the front door before knocking on it.

"Try using this," Susannah suggested, reaching around him to pull on a round brass knob, about two inches large, placed near the right-hand doorjamb. Instantly a bell jangled on the other side of the door.

"How did you know about that?" Kane asked.

"I'm an editor. I know all kinds of things. However, I don't know what makes you think they'll answer the door at this time of night."

"The fact that they're expecting me."

"Oh? Did you call ahead?" she mockingly inquired. "Hold the reservation with your credit card?"

"I just used common sense."

"I didn't know you had any," she muttered.

"There's a lot about me you don't know," Kane retorted. "Good evening," he greeted the woman who cautiously opened the door. "Mrs. Broadstreet? Jed Paines over at the City Tavern said you'd be expecting us. My name is Kane Wilder and this is my wife, Susannah."

"Ah, the poor couple that had their luggage stolen at the train station." Nodding, the white lacy cap on her head tied in place with a prim bow just beneath her jaw, Mrs. Broadstreet opened the door wider in an invitation for them to come inside. "Jed sent a runner over with a note telling me all about it. He said you had an important party to attend and would be coming here directly afterward."

"That's right," Kane confirmed.

"We apologize for the lateness of the hour," Susannah said with unaccustomed formality.

"Well, I don't usually take in boarders without references," Mrs. Broadstreet confessed, "but I trust Jed's judgment. He's got a sixth sense about people."

"Really?" Susannah murmured. "I didn't realize that." Susannah didn't have much faith in Jed's so-called sixth sense. After all, the man had thought she was a street-walker like Polly!

"How dreadful to have all your trunks stolen that way," Mrs. Broadstreet was saying. "At least you were able to save one of your bags." She pointed to Susannah's purse, hanging from her shoulder. "I must confess I've never seen one quite like that before. We're not always up-to-date on the latest fashions here in Savannah, not like they are up in New York, but we do like to think that we keep up with things. About your missing trunks, I do hope you've notified the proper authorities?"

Kane nodded. "They don't hold out much hope of finding our things, though."

"I don't know what the world is coming to," Mrs. Broadstreet exclaimed with a shake of her head. "No one is safe. When the president of the United States can be assassinated in a railway station..."

Kane frowned. "I thought Lincoln was assassinated at a theater."

"I was referring to President Garfield's assassination three years ago."

"Oh."

"You'll have to forgive my husband," Susannah quickly said. "It's been a long day."

Mrs. Broadstreet nodded understandingly. "I'll show you directly to your room, then."

As they followed their landlady upstairs, Kane whispered to Susannah, "It's been a long day, all right. About a hundred and eleven years long!"

"Shh."

On the second floor, Mrs. Broadstreet led them to a room at the end of the hallway. As she prepared to open the door to their room, she said, "You'll be needing some night-clothes. I hope you don't mind my presumptuousness—I already set them out for you on the bed. My daughter left some clothes behind you can borrow, Mrs. Wilder, until your trunks are found. And my departed husband was about your size, Mr. Wilder, so the few things of his that I kept should fit you."

"Thank you," Kane said.

"If you'd like me to have the things you're wearing cleaned, just let me know." Mrs. Broadstreet went on to hesitantly name the amount for a week's room and board. When Kane didn't blink an eyelash, she added, "That would be payable in advance."

Kane reached into his inside jacket pocket and carefully counted out the appropriate amount. The money was totally unfamiliar to him. He'd been careful not to put the nineteenth-century bills in his wallet lest he pulled a crisp twentieth-century greenback out by mistake.

Meanwhile, Susannah was wondering how one asked directions to the ladies' room in 1884. Surely indoor plumbing was around by now? She'd stayed in Victorian bed-and-breakfasts before and they'd always had the most adorable bathrooms. Sometimes they were located down the hall, though.

"Is there a bathroom attached to our room?" she asked hopefully, looking around for a doorway.

"Bathroom?" their landlady repeated in confusion. "We have a copper bathtub in the room at the other end of the hallway."

"What about the toilet? The john?" Susannah tried every description she could think of. She was getting desperate here. She hadn't gone in 111 years!

"There's a convenience out back."

Out back? Susannah briefly wondered if she looked as dismayed as she felt. How could something outside be considered convenient?

"Or, if your prefer, there is that newfangled invention my husband insisted on getting before his untimely death." She opened a door and, holding up the flickering lamp, showed them what she was talking about. "He made me promise to pour a bucket of water down it every few days, but that's all I've done with it."

It was a toilet—the oldest one on record, perhaps, and bearing little resemblance to anything Susannah had seen before, but it *was* a toilet, with a wooden seat and a chain hung from the ceiling.

Misinterpreting Susannah's doubtful look, Mrs. Broadstreet said, "The water comes from a cistern on the roof, and it does work, but I've never quite trusted the thing myself. You hear these stories of sewer-gas explosions and all...."

Kane bent down to study the plumbing. He'd gotten a crash course in old-fashioned plumbing when a friend of his had bought a run-down Victorian house and, for a six-pack and a free dinner, he'd pitched in to help his buddy redo the bathrooms. Standing again, Kane said, "Sewer gas isn't a problem, not with the elbow in the pipe. The standing water there prevents sewer gas from backing up. That's why your husband had you pour water down it, to keep water in that elbow if you weren't using it very often."

"You sound as if you know about such things," Mrs. Broadstreet noted in admiration. "Are you a plumber by any chance?"

"No, ma'am."

"Oh. I'm sorry. I didn't mean to pry. Well, I'll just leave you both to your ablutions, then. There's fresh water in the pitcher in your room. And the lamp is lit. What time would you like breakfast?"

"Nine would be fine."

"All right, then. Good night. Oh, you'll be needing this." Mrs. Broadstreet handed over the kerosene lamp to Susannah.

"What about you?"

"Oh, I could find my way through this house blindfolded," Mrs. Broadstreet told her with a grin as wide as she was. "Good night."

As she carefully closed the water-closet door and made use of the facilities, Susannah told herself that this was no different than the summer vacations she and her family had spent in a rented woodland cabin in upstate New York. The electricity had been iffy and they'd often had to rely on candlelight or kerosene lamps. And while the plumbing may not have been as antiquated as this was, at least this was an *indoor* facility.

The water closet was rather cramped for space—now she knew why it was called a *closet*—so she had to be careful to keep the heavy velvet of her long skirt away from the lamp, which she'd been forced to set on the floor for lack of anyplace else to put it. All she needed at this point was to set fire to herself! Since she didn't see anything resembling toilet paper, she had to use some tissues she had in the side pocket of her ever-present purse. With some trepidation, she pulled the chain, fearing the roof might cave in, but the system worked—much to her relief.

Since there was no sink, a wet towelette, also from her purse, allowed her to clean her hands. She saw no wastebasket in the small enclosure, so she had to stick the soiled towelette in a Ziploc plastic bag and stash it in an inside compartment of her purse until she could dispose of it. She always carried a few bags with her, using them for all kinds of things.

Hoisting her purse back over her shoulder, Susannah carefully picked up the lamp and made her way to the room she'd be sharing with Kane that night.

The room was simply furnished—a double bed, a dresser that had a flowered washbowl and pitcher on top of it and a mirror on the wall behind it, a screen made of some kind of fabric between a wooden frame, and a rocking chair in the corner with what looked like a hand-crocheted pillow on it. The carpet was sisal, she thought, and the walls were papered in a dark maroon print on an oyster white backing. There were no pictures on the walls. Light was furnished by a wall fixture covered with an etched-glass globe.

"Gas," Kane said.

"Do you need an antacid?" she asked, reaching into her purse.

Smiling, Kane shook his head, a lock of his dark brown hair falling over his forehead. "I was referring to the light. It's gas."

"Oh." She eyed the lamp fixture suspiciously. While Mrs. Broadstreet might be afraid of sewer gas, Susannah wasn't real fond of natural gas, due to an explosion that had occurred in their neighborhood when she was a child. A construction worker with a backhoe had inadvertently hit a gas main, rupturing it. Two people had been badly injured in the resultant explosion. Her mother had immediately gone out and bought an electric stove. Susannah had electric in her first two apartments, as well.

"How do you turn it off?" she asked suspiciously.

"With that valve on the bottom." Kane came closer to show her what he was talking about. "The premise is the same as turning off your stove."

"I have an electric stove at home." *Home.* The word hit her with the force of a ton of bricks. When would she be home again? When would she see her family again? She didn't realize she'd voiced the question aloud until Kane said, "I don't know when we'll get back."

"It was Wednesday when we left.... I wasn't supposed to fly back to New York until Tuesday morning. But my absence from the conference is going to be noted before that." And not appreciated, Susannah added to herself. Knowing McPhearson Publishing's coldhearted personnel policy, she doubted that "time travel" was in the manual as an excuse for unauthorized leave. She could just imagine herself trying to explain things to her boss. It wouldn't go over well at all. She could almost hear him saying, "We've all got problems, but we don't let them interfere with our work."

"I'll be missed, too," Kane said, interrupting her thoughts.

"Leave a girlfriend back home, did you?" The words were out of her mouth before she could stop them.

"I meant missed at work," he replied.

"Oh. I meant the same thing. And I'll be missed by my family."

"Same here."

So there was no girlfriend for him back home. Interesting. "How do you think this time-travel thing works? Do you think that time is going on back there as it is here?"

Kane shook his head. "If you'd have asked me that question yesterday, I'd have said that a situation like this was impossible. But clearly it is possible. From what I remember about Einstein's theory, time is progressing at an equal pace. Damn, I wish I had my laptop with me! I could access that information in an instant. But who knew when I left the hotel this evening, that I'd end up here?"

"Don't tell me you're helpless without your computer? Let me guess, I'll bet you don't know anyone's phone number, either. Only their number on your memory bank. Am I right?"

As if on cue, his watch chimed again.

"Boys and their toys," she murmured with a shake of her head.

"I'll have you know this watch stores thirty different phone numbers, can be set for sixty different alarm settings, and shows the time in twenty-seven cities worldwide."

She wasn't impressed. "So what? It's not going to do you any good here."

"I wouldn't say that. It helped me win at tonight's card game."

"Even so, you'd better take it off before anyone else notices how strange it is." Squinting at it, she said, "How can you even read it with all those little dials and things on there?"

"I'm not taking it off, but I will turn the alarm function off."

Realizing that was as much of a compromise as she was likely to get from him, she went on to the next item on her agenda. "Listen, after your comment about Lincoln, I think perhaps I should fill you in on a few important basics regarding this time period. As I said, I edited a book on the Victorian era not too long ago. I'll try and go over a few of the high points. The period is named after Queen Victoria, of course."

"I know that much," he said irritably.

"Well, actually it's better known as the Gilded Age in this country. Mark Twain gave it that label, as I recall. And he wasn't being complimentary. This is the start of a period of excessive consumption and a ruthless pursuit of profit."

"Sounds like the 1980s," Kane noted.

Susannah nodded. "There are a lot of similarities, actually. Both were periods of great innovation and invention. Electricity, the telephone, moving pictures, recordings—all these things come about in this era."

"The same way computers and cellular communications and other technologies were developed in the seventies and eighties of our century."

"That's right. There was also a lot of fraud among the bigwigs. Fortunes were made and lost. The stock market was manipulated."

"Sounds like Ivan Boesky and the junk-bonds scandal. So who is the president of the United States now?"

"Arthur."

"Arthur who?"

"Chester A. Arthur."

"Get out of here. I don't remember anything about a President Arthur. How can we have had a president I didn't even know anything about?" Kane demanded, clearly not liking the feeling of being at an intellectual disadvantage.

"He wasn't all that memorable. The poor man didn't even get his own party's nomination to run for president again. He only had the three years in office, after Garfield's assassination, because he was vice president."

"Jeez, and Bush thought *he* had it bad."

"Let me see, what else can I tell you . . . ?"

"Baseball was around."

She nodded. "And Mark Twain's *The Prince and the Pauper* is out. I heard it being discussed at the party tonight."

"In which century?" he wryly inquired.

"This one. Which brings us back to the big question."

"Why are we here?"

"And where are the cookies?" she couldn't resist adding. At his startled look, she said, "Sorry. It's just that I've got a T-shirt at home that says—The Big Questions— Who Am I? Why Am I Here? Where Are the Cookies?"

Kane groaned. "Don't mention food. I never did get that burger I was looking for."

"I think I have some food in my purse." Digging around, she was delighted to find the apple she'd bought and stashed from the convention center, a travel-size package of cookies, two candy bars, a roll of candy Life Savers, a handful of saltines, several salted-nut packages, a package of sugar-free gum, a roll of breath mints, and some kind of dried trail mix advertising a new backpacking book coming out next year. She'd taken the plastic container holding a salad out of her purse earlier while still back at the hotel. Laying her findings out on top of the dresser, she said, "I'm willing to share."

Kane looked at the assortment of food in amusement.

"I bring candy on the plane so I don't get airsick," she said rather defensively. "And I never eat the salted nuts they give you until later, because while you're flying the salt just makes you bloat more."

For some reason she blushed. Talking about bloating made her feel self-conscious—as if she were the size of a hot-air balloon.

She didn't care what he thought. She was starving. She reached for the apple.

Kane took one of the candy bars and a few saltines. "I didn't get a chance to actually count my winnings—"

"Our winnings," she interrupted him before taking another bite of the crisp apple.

Staring at Susannah, her eyes closed with pleasure as she ate, Kane was reminded of Eve and all the temptations she presented Adam. Susannah could have posed for a portrait of Eve—dressed as she was in that red velvet gown. The material was as soft as her skin. The intense color made her creamy skin all the more beautiful.

But like Eve, she was dangerous to a man's peace of mind. She was responsible for almost ruining his brother's marriage and Kane would do well not to forget that fact.

Returning his attention to the money he'd spread out on the bed, Kane concentrated on counting it. First he had to figure out what was what. Nothing looked familiar! The coins he had went from a penny up to a ten-dollar gold piece.

The paper money was larger than he was accustomed to...but wait! There was good ol' George Washington on the face of a dollar bill! Finally, a friendly face! The back side of the bill looked weird, but no weirder than jumping centuries was. Kane's grin faded as he realized he had no idea of the current value of these denominations—it was hard to get a rate of exchange for a currency a century old. When he'd traveled to Europe, there had been signs showing the conversion rate. He wasn't going to get that kind of help here.

Sitting in the rocking chair, Susannah ignored Kane and decided to do an inventory of her purse. The two largest items were the portable cassette player—a godsend on the plane to keep the noise of the engines from giving her a headache—and her makeup bag with essentials like a toothbrush and travel-size toothpaste, deodorant and bubble bath. When packing she always threw last-minute stuff into her purse, basically whatever didn't fit into her carry-on garment bag. Which meant she often had an unusual combination of things left over in her purse after flying. Normally she dumped the extra junk in her hotel room, but there hadn't been time tonight. Thank heaven!

What else was in there . . . ? Her jumble of keys with the personal alarm attached to the key chain. That could prove useful. Then she found something even more useful—an extra pair of underwear! A friend of hers in the lingerie business had given her a travel pair—rolled up into a capsule the size of those prizes they used to have in gum-ball machines. Susannah valued this find as if it were a prize, for it meant she could wash out the pair she was wearing—both were made of fast-drying nylon. With two pairs of underwear, she was well armed to face the world.

Digging into her purse again, her hands closed on the round bottle that held her prescription medication. Discreetly flipping it open inside her purse, she took stock.

"If we budget our money we should do okay for about a month," Kane said from the other side of the room.

"A month!" Susannah looked up from her pill counting. "We can't stay a month! I've only got sixteen days' worth of pills with me." The words slipped out of her mouth.

"What kind of pills?" Kane demanded suspiciously.

"None of your business," she muttered.

"Great. I get stuck time-traveling with some pill-popping junkie!"

She could have told him about her heart condition, which didn't prevent her from leading a normal life providing that she stayed on the medication, but his attitude had evaporated any desire to tell him a thing. "You know, the first time I met you, I thought you were an idiot. I was wrong. You're a stupid, barbaric, ill-mannered idiot!"

With that declaration, she grabbed the thin cotton nightdress from the foot of the bed and stalked over to the screen near the dresser. She'd inadvertently brought her purse with her. Fine. She didn't trust him with it anyway. She wouldn't put it past him to snitch her remaining candy bar, not to mention her cassette tape player.

"Uh, Susannah..."

"I'm not speaking to you," she frostily informed him, undoing the side zipper on her velvet dress before pulling the bulky thing off over her head. Ah, that felt better. A warm breeze came in through the shuttered windows, the wooden louvers aimed in such a way that she was able to feel the movement of air. It provided a welcome relief.

But she still felt sticky. Glancing at the washbowl and pitcher, she decided to take a short sponge bath. Pouring some of the water into the washbowl, she undid her bra and used the corner of a linen hand towel as a washcloth along with some soap, which she'd snitched from the airplane bathroom, to wash. The water was deliciously cool against her skin and she relished the interlude, taking her time. Feeling refreshed, she dried off with a larger towel before sliding the nightgown on over her head. She also slipped on the new pair of bikini underwear, a leopard print she'd never have chosen for herself. The white pair she'd just removed were washed and hung to dry in as discreet a location as she could find. Ditto with her panty hose. The soapy water from the washbowl, she figured out, got poured into a bucket left on the floor for that purpose.

When she finally came from behind the cover provided by the screen, she found Kane lying on the bed. He'd taken off his jacket, undone his shirt, and was resting with his arms beneath his head, staring at the screen with a huge grin on his face.

Following his gaze, she only then realized that the light of the lamp on the dresser beside the screen had turned the white material into a see-through shadow show, allowing him to see her every move and every contour while she'd changed clothes! Susannah saw red.

"You dirty pervert!" Yanking the pillow out from under his head, she whacked him on the stomach with it.

The pillow, filled with heavy feathers, was no lightweight thing and the whoosh of his breath exhaling told her that she'd made a direct hit. Good! She hoped he'd think twice before playing the role of a Peeping Tom again.

Kane didn't appear to show any remorse, however. Instead, he looked as angry as she felt. Growling, he grabbed hold of her wrist and yanked her toward him. Next thing Susannah knew, she was falling....

# Four

Susannah's descent was abruptly halted by Kane's half-naked chest—upon which she lay sprawled, momentarily at a loss for words. When she'd fallen on top of him, he'd gasped for breath. So had she.

Before she'd lost her balance, Susannah had seen the startling flame of hunger in Kane's blue eyes. Now she couldn't see anything. Her eyes were closed but her other sensory pathways were wide open and being bombarded with intimate details. He'd already removed his suit jacket. The thin material of her borrowed nightgown and his rented shirt and pants did little to conceal the warmth emanating from their bodies—a warmth that was increased by the sudden awareness striking sparks between them.

In an instant, the memory of his kiss earlier that evening came back to her with vivid detail. Her nose was pressed into the hollow of his throat and she could feel his Adam's apple move as he swallowed. Her hands were trapped beneath her, sandwiched between her chest and his. She could feel the beat of his heart against her palm. It was racing. So was hers.

She felt frozen, like an insect trapped in amber. Her mind knew she should move, should push away immediately, but her body seemed to lag behind—like a caboose on a long freight train. Her hips were pressed against his and there was no mistaking his very male reaction to having her sprawled atop him like this. Or had he already been aroused from watching her undress behind that screen?

The thought sped up her reflexes. Using her hands to prop herself up, she found herself looking down at his face, directly into his eyes. They sloped downward on the outside corners, giving him a bedroom look. Of course, she *was* in a bedroom with him, on the bed with him, reacting to him. The expression in his blue eyes caught her and threw her off-balance as surely as his grip around her wrist had done moments before.

Where had that hunger come from? Was she looking at him the same way? God, she hoped not! But chances were that she was. Because she felt the gnawing yearning to get even closer than she was, to lower her lips to his, to once again feel the sensual intensity of his kiss.

She wasn't sure if he moved, or if she did. She only knew that his mouth was covering hers. Whereas their previous kiss had been sudden and intense, this one was slow and sweet. She was drawn into it, became an equal participant in the seductive swirl of tongues.

Wait, this couldn't be, *mustn't* be! She struggled to free herself from the magically hazy web that held her in its grip while forcibly reminding herself that Kane had accused her of having an affair with his brother. He thought she was a loose woman. He was not good for her. Something to be avoided.

Avoidance was difficult to do while they were sharing this bedroom, however. The first step was to end this bewitching kiss. She did so immediately. Her eyes met his for a second before she tore her gaze from his, for the first time noticing the white mosquito netting draped from the canopy and tied back at the corners of the four-poster bed.

Susannah's thoughts of passion went out the proverbial window as another thought occurred to her—regarding windows without screens... mosquitoes... and yellow fever.

"Wait a second.... When did they get rid of yellow fever?" she demanded of Kane even as she scrambled off the bed.

"Wha-at?" He was clearly startled by her question. One minute he'd been holding a soft bundle of femininity in his arms, with brown eyes the color of chocolate and lips that could make a blind man see, and the next instant she was shooting questions at him about yellow fever. Did she think he was sick or something?

Maybe he *was* sick—that would explain the fever he felt whenever she was near. She was getting under his skin. That first kiss back at the poker table had almost knocked his socks off. He could understand why his younger brother, Chuck, had fallen for her. Susannah was a passionate woman. Voluptuous. When he'd just kissed her now, her full breasts had pressed against his chest like soft pillows and his hands had itched to cup them, to brush his thumbs over the nipples he could feel through the thin material of her nightgown....

"Yellow fever," Susannah demanded in an attention-grabbing voice. "When did they find a cure for it?"

Pushing away his erotic thoughts, Kane switched mental gears and searched his memory. "While building the Panama Canal, I think."

"Yes, but what year?"

"Damned if I know," he said irritably, still ticked off by the way he'd reacted to her.

"Then there's no way I'm sleeping on the floor and risking getting bitten by a germ-infested mosquito!" she declared.

"So you want to sleep with me?" he drawled.

The knowing look in his eyes provoked her anger instead of her passion. "I find it only slightly less appealing than having yellow fever," she retorted. "And I wouldn't be *sleeping* with you."

"We'd be doing something else in this bed?"

Kane was deliberately making things difficult for her and she was tempted to whack him with the twenty-pound pillow again. "We would be sharing the bed. That's it. Nothing else. It's big enough for both of us. And we could roll up this quilt and put it between us, it's certainly too warm to use it for anything else." She pounced on the quilt as if it were a long-lost possession.

"Aren't you a little overdressed for sleeping?" Kane mockingly inquired.

"This is as undressed as I'm getting," she stated coolly. The nightgown covered her practically from neck to ankles, and while she would have preferred the short silk chemise nightie packed in her suitcase back at the hotel, she didn't have that option.

"Do you plan on wearing your necklace to bed?" Kane asked.

Looking down, she realized he was right. She was still wearing the garnet necklace originally belonging to her great-grandmother. In fact, she was still wearing all her jewelry.

"Afraid I'm going to steal it?" he inquired dryly. "I can assure you that you don't have anything I want."

Her look called him a liar.

So he rephrased his observation. "Let me put it this way. You don't have anything I care to take. Of course, if you're *giving* anything away..."

"You already got the only thing you're getting from me. One candy bar!"

"And a few saltines, not to mention two kisses."

"I'd rather you didn't mention those kisses. And don't repeat them, either," she warned him with a chilly look, before removing her garnet jewelry set and stashing it in a quilted-silk holder she had in her purse. "You caught me off guard, otherwise you'd have been bent over and talking funny for a week. I do know how to protect myself, you know."

"I'm impressed," he said in a voice that made her doubt he meant a word of it—although the look he was giving her *did* give the impression he was impressed, but not by her self-defense abilities. He was eyeing her as if trying to paint a mental picture of what she looked like under the concealing cotton of her nightgown.

"I think we should be concentrating on what our next course of action will be regarding our situation," she stated firmly.

"You're talking . . . quaintly again. And I thought we already decided what our next course of action would be— that you're going to be sleeping with me."

She glared at him, but otherwise ignored his comment. "I was referring to Elsbeth. Clearly we need to find out more about her, since she's the key to all of this. She's the one who brought us back. Now we have to figure out why."

"I'm still having a hard time buying this time-travel thing," Kane admitted.

"Really? Don't tell me you plan on walking into any more streetlamp poles," she drawled.

He didn't look amused. "I'm hoping to wake up in the morning and find I'm back in my hotel room, because frankly I don't have time for any of this," he growled.

"Time is something you can't control. I think we're excellent examples of that fact," she countered.

He made no reply, simply loosened the remaining buttons on his shirt and closed his eyes.

"Aren't you going to get undressed?" she asked.

He popped one eye open to lazily inform her, "Nope. No floor show tonight. Turn out the light."

The man was impossible! "Turn it off yourself," she muttered, focusing her attention on placing the thickly rolled-up quilt in the middle of the bed—from headboard to footboard.

While Kane got up to turn down the gaslight, Susannah quickly scrambled into bed, pulling the mosquito netting on her side down before tucking it in beneath the mattress so that there were no openings for the bloodsucking little devils to work their way in.

However, once the lamp was out and darkness filled the room, Susannah found she couldn't sleep. The reality of her situation was sinking in—but good!

Kane was sound asleep; she could hear his rhythmic breathing—almost a snore but not quite. Restful respite failed her, however. Kane was right: she *was* starting to talk and even think like a Victorian.

And like any proper Victorian miss, she was on the verge of having a fit of the vapors. Or was that a Regency expression? Whatever, she felt like having a major crying jag. Here she was, stuck in 1884 with the last man on earth with whom she wanted to share company—let alone share a bed!

She felt lost and alone. Marooned. Tears threatened at the back of her throat and eyes.

She hadn't felt this weepy since a disastrous trip down to St. Martin last year—to a resort that hadn't even finished being constructed, let alone matched the shiny brochures. She'd held up pretty well then, taking the hole in the roof, the broken air-conditioning, the backed-up toilet, with a stoic stiff upper lip. But when she'd turned out the light and seen beady lizard eyes, a dozen of them, glowing at her from the hole in the roof, Susannah had lost her composure. She felt like that now. On the verge of losing her composure.

Oh, hell, who was she kidding? She'd lost her composure some time ago—probably from that first moment when she'd walked out of the historic Whitaker house and had a bad feeling. She'd lost even more when she'd read the nineteenth-century date on that circus handbill posted to the lamppost.

While the idea of time travel might sound romantic and exciting, she had to admit that the reality was downright...scary. This was completely unknown territory for her, and she wasn't real fond of unknown territory.

Okay, so she knew *something* about the time period, at least. But she was certainly no expert. She didn't even know when yellow fever had been cured, for cripes' sake. That information would have come in mighty handy tonight.

So what *was* she doing here? Most time-travel claims she'd heard or read about seemed to revolve around big historical events, like the Civil War or the American Revolution. Now that Susannah thought about it, no doubt that was a similar phenomenon to so many people believing they'd been Cleopatra or someone equally famous in a previous life. Everyone wanted to be a major player. No one wanted to get lost in the shuffle.

Susannah had ended up in a shuffle, all right—a time shuffle. But did *she* end up in the midst of historical actions of monumental consequence? No, of course not. She ended up on a quiet street in Victorian Savannah, sharing a bed with a man who kissed like the devil and was sure to drive her nuts.

Okay, so she was grateful not to have landed in worse times. But given this time period, she could have ended up in the Vanderbilts' Fifth Avenue mansion—that might not have been too hard to take. Or she could have ended up in one of New York City's many tenement buildings. Or in a sod house out in the middle of Nebraska. There was such a great diversity in American life-styles during this decade— the Western frontier still in its formative stages while New York City was rapidly becoming the most crowded place on the planet. Some days on the subway in her own time period, the city still felt that way.

Even so, Susannah longed to be back on that familiar crowded subway. Biting her lip to hold back the tears, eventually she decided that perhaps the best way to deal with this lost feeling was the way she dealt with the hassles at-

tached to living in New York City. She marched right on, as
if she knew exactly what she was doing, the look on her face
daring anyone to give her a hard time. If it worked on
Manhattan's subway, certainly it would work in Victorian
times? Weren't they supposed to be gentler times?

*You need to help me.*

The words stole into her consciousness. She could hear
them as if they'd been clearly spoken. But she heard them
inside her own head.

"Elsbeth?" Susannah whispered uncertainly, exhaustion
catching up with her, washing over her and tugging her into
slumber's arms.

*Don't be afraid.*

Remembering that any communication with the ghost had
been cut off the last time she'd attempted to speak aloud,
Susannah used her thoughts to talk to her. *Elsbeth, why am
I here?*

*To help me.*

Susannah struggled to keep her thoughts together. She
was so tired. . . . *But I can't help you. We got here too late.*

*No. You can still help me. Clear my name.*

The idea crept into Susannah's consciousness just before
she finally fell deep asleep to dream of a man with blue eyes
and a gambler's smile.

Susannah woke slowly the next morning with no clear
idea where she was or what was going on. Had she been
dreaming she'd jumped centuries? Had a ghost really talked
to her? In that hazy world between waking and sleeping, she
blearily opened her eyes. She saw nothing but white. Brilliant, blinding white.

Thoughts hit her brain with lightning speed. Had she
died? Her heart dropped, no wait . . . it must not be beating
in the first place—not if she was dead.

She vastly preferred the time-travel angle to being dead.

At least she was in heaven. White denoted that, right?
Although, come to think of it, it certainly was hotter than

Hades. Surely she hadn't ended up...elsewhere? For what? Lying on her driver's-license application? No one put their true weight on that damn form!

"Are you going to lie there all day or are you going to get up?"

Startled, Susannah flipped onto her back and stared at Kane. "You!"

"You were expecting someone else in your bed?"

Bed... The white she'd seen must have been mosquito netting! "I wasn't expecting—"

"Dreaming about my married brother, were you?" he interrupted her, his voice hard. Susannah looked too damn inviting in the morning. She'd looked sexy as hell in the middle of the night when he'd gotten up to remove his shirt and slacks, sleeping only in his shorts. He'd woken this morning to find her curled against him, the quilt she'd insisted on using as a divider somehow having been kicked to the foot of the bed. She'd felt so soft and appealing. In sleep, her face was as angelic as a child's. Yet the attraction he'd felt for her had been completely adult.

Kane couldn't allow himself to fall for her tricks. So he'd leapt out of bed as if bitten by a snake, while Susannah had merely rolled onto her other side and gone on sleeping.

"I was not dreaming about your brother," she hotly denied, wondering if that could actually have been a note of *jealousy* she'd heard in his voice a moment earlier. "If you must know, I thought..." Her voice trailed off as, in the clear light of day, she was reluctant to admit she'd been confused and panicked enough to briefly think she'd died. She could just imagine what he'd make of that. "Never mind. You wouldn't understand. It's hot in here."

"Excuse me, princess, for not turning on the air conditioner," he drawled with a mocking little bow in her direction.

"Very funny."

"I'll tell you what's funny. These clothes." He pointed to the borrowed pants he was wearing. "These don't have a zipper. They have a button fly."

At his having said that, her eyes naturally strayed to the fly of his pants. How could they not, after what he'd just said? The pants fit him loosely, but not loosely enough that she couldn't tell what was beneath the material. He had narrow hips and wide shoulders. Her eyes slid upward to his face, where she saw him smiling smugly at her. "Enjoying the view?" he inquired.

"Not really," she denied. "I was merely studying the clothing. I bet zippers haven't been invented yet."

Picking up his rented slacks, Kane absently noted, "I bet there's a fortune to be had for the guy that does invent the zipper. Maybe I should—"

"Don't even think about it," she interjected, climbing out of the mosquito-netted bed. "You're not stealing the invention from whoever did come up with the idea."

"That wasn't what I was suggesting. I was going to say maybe I should wear the slacks I came in, instead of these things."

"And how do you propose to explain that zipper on there?"

"What makes you think anyone will be looking at my fly?" he countered.

"Trust me, someone will notice."

"Then what do you suggest I do?"

"Keep your pants on. The ones you're wearing, I mean."

"They're awfully loose. I didn't find any belt. Just these things." He held up a pair of suspenders and batted his baby blues at her.

She eyed him suspiciously, not putting it past him to pretend not to know how to use suspenders just to get her to do them up for him. "There should be a button somewhere on the waistband of the pants. Just fasten the open loop at the bottom of the suspenders over it."

He put them on backward, just to aggravate her, no doubt. She should have let him go out that way. Instead, she redid them properly, trying to keep a cushion of air between them. It didn't help minimize the effect of being so close to him, her fingers trapped between the waistband of his pants and the linen shirt. It was last night all over again, and an all-too-familiar forbidden heat stole through her.

His slow gambler's smile let her know that he was aware of her discomfort. To pay him back, she sharply snapped the suspenders against his chest.

"Hey!" he protested.

"Hay is for horses, straw is cheaper," she retorted with an old-fashioned idiom her grandmother had often used. "Mrs. Broadstreet offered to clean our clothes," she reminded him, "but I don't think that's a good idea. I think we should keep them out of sight. Stuff them under the bed. Or carefully fold them and put them under the bed. You may need to wear them again."

"Not to mention returning them to the rental place that owns them," he told her.

"Oh, my gosh, I hadn't even thought of that. I bet we're still being charged for these clothes." She groaned at the idea.

"I'd say we have bigger things to worry about at the moment. But first, don't you think you should get dressed? It's eight-thirty already, and we're supposed to have breakfast at nine."

"I would have gotten dressed faster if you'd been able to put your own suspenders on," she retorted even as she hurried over and gathered the pile of clothing Mrs. Broadstreet had lent her. "I won't be long," she said before slipping behind the dressing screen. This time she made sure where the light—in this case, sunlight—was coming from so that he couldn't observe her every move.

It took her five minutes to figure out what item of clothing went where, before even attempting to put it on. Even though she'd edited a book about this era, reading about it and actually wearing the stuff were two different matters. She put on almost everything their landlady had left for her, skipping only the corset, preferring to use her own bra instead. Same with the underwear. The next layer was a muslin chemise and a god-awful-looking bustle.

"Three hours a week spent on moronic stair machine to minimize my buns and here I am wearing something that makes that part of my anatomy look even larger than it already is," Susannah grumbled under her breath.

She felt a little less ridiculous once she'd put on the final layer of clothing—a blouse, which was white and had long puffy sleeves, and a lovely blue skirt that did button around her waist, for which she was grateful. She put on the cotton stockings provided, which were actually more like long socks. There were no shoes provided, so she wore the black velvet flats she'd put on in 1995. At least *they* were comfortable.

"What's taking you so long?" Kane impatiently demanded from the other side of the room.

"Getting dressed in this time period is harder than it is in my day," she admitted as she stepped from behind the screen, still trying to do up the tiny buttons on the cuff of her borrowed blouse. There was a formfitting red jacket to match the skirt, but the fact that it must be eighty degrees outside prompted Susannah to put off wearing that for the time being. She knew she wouldn't be allowed out of the house without putting it on, however.

Reaching into her purse, she removed her makeup bag and stood in front of the mirror on top of the dresser. She looked as pale as Elsbeth's ghost. Although proper ladies might not wear makeup in this day and age, she needed something.... A discreet dash of mascara helped, as did the old-fashioned remedy of pinching her cheeks and biting her lips. She'd already used deodorant while dressing, and now she made use of her toothbrush.

"Toothpaste!" Kane exclaimed, spying what she had in her hand. "You've got toothpaste! Where did you get it?"

"A drugstore on the Upper East Side."

Kane eyed the tube longingly. "I don't suppose you'd be willing to share some of it?"

She should have turned him down flat. She was sure if the shoe were on the other foot, he'd turn her down. Or make some outrageous suggestion about what he'd want in exchange for the toothpaste. An idea occurred to her....

"I'd be willing to share, providing you don't make any more rude allegations regarding your brother and myself," she offered.

"Allegations?"

"You know what I mean."

"You're still denying that you had an affair with my brother?"

"I'm categorically denying it. I have been since I first heard you make the ridiculous suggestion."

"So you're asking me to abandon my belief in my brother's honesty for a dab of toothpaste?"

Put that way, it did sound rather shallow. But she stuck to her guns. "If we're going to be stuck in such close quarters, it would be much easier if we weren't at each other's throats all the time."

"Oh, I don't know," Kane murmured, his voice suddenly darkly sexy. "You've got a lovely throat...." His gaze went to her creamy skin, visible at the opening of her blouse, the top two buttons of which she'd left undone.

She was so shaken by his gaze, not to mention the passionate implication in his voice, that she almost squeezed the toothpaste tube in half. As it was, she tore her eyes away from his and made a point of not looking at him as she focused on braiding her hair and pinning it at the back of her head before putting on her great-grandmother's garnet jewelry set again.

As she was putting the toothpaste away, she found a small tube of a combined sunscreen/insect-repellent she didn't even know she had. Since it was only a sample size, she'd have to use it sparingly.

And since she didn't want Kane dying or getting sick on her, leaving her alone to cope with nineteenth-century culture shock, she offered him the sample tube, as well. She needed to be able to talk to someone who knew about World War II, President Kennedy, Reaganomics, the Beatles, Princess Di, Bill and Hillary. "You can use some of this, too," she added.

"Without having to sell my soul for it?" Kane inquired mockingly.

"Do you want it or not?"

"Thanks," he said grudgingly.

"If the mosquitoes don't kill you, thanking me will, huh?" she noted with a grin.

Kane made no reply, for he already knew he was in more danger from Susannah and her passionate sensuality than from any damn mosquito. He had to do something, had to stay focused on getting out of this mess.

"You're right," he said abruptly. "It would be easier if we called a temporary truce. We've got our hands full trying to figure out what we're doing here and how to get back to our own time zone. I'm willing to table the issue of my brother until then. What do you say?"

"I agree. We've got enough other things to worry about at the moment." Things like yellow fever, not to mention her feverish attraction to Kane. Yes, Susannah had enough other things to worry about, all right!

"Good morning," Mrs. Broadstreet greeted them at the bottom of the stairs. "I trust you both slept well?"

"Yes, thanks," Kane replied.

"Actually, I was a bit concerned about yellow fever," Susannah began as their landlady led them into the dining room.

"Oh, visitations of yellow fever have been rare in this area. We haven't had anything lately such as they had up in Memphis several years back. The sea breeze here is most wholesome."

"How reassuring."

"The outbreaks of fever have been much reduced since the time when I was a girl," Mrs. Broadstreet went on to say.

"I'm glad I didn't visit earlier, then," Susannah noted dryly.

"I hope you're hungry. I've had a nice breakfast prepared for you."

Actually, Susannah was dying for a bagel and cream cheese but she smiled her appreciation for the effort Mrs. Broadstreet had gone to. The meal was huge, and was a fried breakfast similar to those she'd been served when she'd visited England a few years back. Only this breakfast had ham and grits as well as eggs. All fried in butter or lard, no doubt. Her cholesterol level would go through the roof at this rate!

The coffee was good, hot and strong. And the jam in the jam pot was homemade, as was the bread, which was delicious. Susannah stuck to bread and jam, nibbling on her fried eggs and ham enough not to appear rude. The grits she couldn't manage at this time of morning. No doubt they were an acquired taste.

A maid, in a plain black dress and white apron, served them. She acted as if she didn't speak much English, and was not the most graceful of people. When the maid broke a glass after almost dropping a plate, Mrs. Broadstreet moaned and confessed, "It's hard to get good help these days. They take off as quickly as they come. That's enough, Gerta," she said as the maid began to weep noisily. "You may go back to the kitchen."

As Mrs. Broadstreet efficiently cleared the rest of the table, Susannah couldn't help noticing the older woman's discreet stares at the fingernail polish Susannah was wearing. She'd been eyeing her nails ever since Susannah had first sat down at the table.

When Kane engrossed himself in the newspaper that had been placed beside his dish, Mrs. Broadstreet finally couldn't resist asking Susannah, "Did you injure yourself that your nails are all red like that?"

"No. They're painted that color." And her with no nail-polish remover.

"I've never heard of such a thing," Mrs. Broadstreet murmured.

"It's the latest fashion." Having said that, Susannah got up from her chair almost to fall over it due to her lack of mobility in the tight skirt. Seeing Mrs. Broadstreet's confused look, Susannah felt compelled to explain, "Er, I'm more accustomed to hoopskirts."

"Well, I do have a trunkful of those up in the attic. You may borrow one of those, if you'd prefer. I'll get Mikey to bring the trunks with those old gowns down and you may try them, see if they fit."

"But not right now," Kane announced, clearly impatient to be going. "We're already late for our appointment. We really do have to hit the road—I mean, get moving. Leave."

"I'm ready," Susannah declared, reluctantly putting on the accompanying coat to her outfit. At this rate, maybe she'd sweat the extra calories off!

"Don't forget your hat. I've got one you may borrow," Mrs. Broadstreet added. "And I've got a bowler here for Mr. Wilder."

After putting on the formfitting jacket, Susannah eyed the hat warily. It had a broad brim and required a hatpin to hold it in place. The feathers and ribbons were quieter than they could have been. Susannah seemed to recall reading about some hats during this period that were actually decorated with *real* flowers and birds, complete with bird's nest.

As for Kane, he looked quite dashing in his bowler.

"Don't forget this," Mrs. Broadstreet added, handing Susannah a fawn-colored silk parasol.

On the front steps, Kane muttered, "I thought we'd never get out of there."

"What are you complaining about? I'm the one who has to wear this ridiculous bustle," Susannah grumbled.

"It was...*big* of you, I must say," he returned with a grin and a telling look at her derriere.

She was tempted to whack his arm with her parasol, but didn't want to break the lovely accessory, with its carved wooden handle. Besides, it served some practical purpose, keeping the sun's rays off her. She was hot enough as it was, with so many layers of clothing on.

This was the first time she'd been outside in daylight since reaching this century, and Susannah couldn't help looking around in amazement. There was so much to see! A street vendor stood at the corner, selling fruits and nuts from a handcart. A woman, with a homemade shopping basket over her arm, was looking over his wares. People seemed to move at two speeds—sweeping past or strolling along. There were plenty of dresses fuller than Susannah's, but they were worn around the hems, and the colors seemed faded, reminding her that the South was still economically recovering from the Civil War.

The smells were as unusual a combination as the sights were: flowers, horse manure, and salty sea air. She heard a little boy laughing as he chased after a puppy in the nearby park.

Savannah seemed to be a city on the move; carriages, wagons, drays and buckboards passed by with every imaginable load—from ice to furniture. Without the distraction of concrete and asphalt, the city's natural foliage became even more evident—the moss-hung oak trees, the palmettos, the magnolias and the delightful oleander bushes.

A slight breeze made the humid heat a little more bearable, but still left Susannah wondering how all these people survived the high temperatures without benefit of shorts or tank tops. Many of the men were wearing white suits, which helped deflect the sun's rays. As it was, Susannah was grateful for her parasol and was amazed at how the mere act of holding it balanced against her shoulder made her feel like a Victorian lady.

"Okay, so now what do we do?" she asked Kane as they began leisurely strolling down the street.

"Return to the Whitaker house and get some answers," he said.

"How do you propose we get in?"

"We could try knocking at the door."

"At which time a servant will open it, and want to see a calling card. Somehow I don't think that my business card or yours will be appropriate in this situation."

"Why do I get the impression you're not talking about my AT&T card when you're referring to a calling card?" he noted dryly.

"These people were sticklers for protocol. I may not be an expert on the clothing of this age, but I can tell you that anyone who was anyone had a calling card with his name printed on it."

"So we tell whoever opens the door that our calling cards were stolen along with our luggage."

"And that we've asked a printer to make up more," she supplied. "That might work." She touched her garnet necklace, which lay on top of her blouse, for good luck. "Okay, let's do it."

They did, only to be told by the servant who opened the door at the Whitaker house that no one was at home. The servant also seemed to be fascinated by Susannah's necklace, which he openly stared at before quickly catching himself.

"Where is Mr. Whitaker? It's important that we speak to him," Kane stated.

"We've come a long way," Susannah added.

The servant paused as if trying to make up his mind about something. Then he said, "The master is at his law office." He gave them the address.

When Susannah and Kane reached Hayward Whitaker's law office, there was an impressive brass sign outside bearing his name. Inside was an outer office, but there was no one sitting at the large desk placed there. So they went on to the next doorway…and walked in on a man on the verge of embracing a woman with red hair.

"I'm sorry," Susannah hurriedly apologized. "We were looking for Mr. Whitaker."

"I am Mr. Whitaker."

"Mr. Hayward Whitaker?"

"That's correct."

No, it wasn't, Susannah thought to himself. It wasn't correct at all, for Mr. Hayward Whitaker didn't look to her like a man who'd lost his wife a mere month ago.

As if thinking the same thing, Kane whispered to her in an aside, "The plot thickens."

# Five

---

"I told you, I'm Hayward Whitaker. Now who the devil are you?" the man angrily demanded, his bearded jowls quivering like jelly. "And what do you mean by barging in here unannounced?"

"I'm sorry, but there was no one at the desk outside," Susannah told him.

"Stevens, get in here!" Hayward bellowed. Going to the door, he looked at the empty desk and muttered, "Blasted clerk is never there when I need him."

"I must be going," his red-haired female companion said in a whispery voice. Grabbing hold of her extravagant hat, which was sitting on Hayward's paper-covered desk, she made a hurried exit, leaving the scent of her tea-rose perfume behind.

Turning to face them, Hayward said, "State your purpose and be quick about it. I'm a busy man."

Then his gaze landed on Susannah's necklace and his face

paled before turning as red as the garnets. "Where did you get that?"

Susannah lifted her hand to cover her necklace, as if fearing he'd yank it off her. How should she answer that question? That her great-grandmother had left it to her? That wouldn't do at all. Deciding the best defense was a good offense, she turned his question back at him. "What makes you ask?"

"Because I happen to know that the design is a one-of-a-kind and was made by a jeweler in New York for my wife and a dear friend of hers."

"And was that lovely lady that just left your wife?" Kane asked, hoping to throw the other man.

Hayward's face darkened. "No, she is not. My dearly departed wife is . . . no longer with us."

Sensing Hayward's anger was about to explode, Susannah hurriedly said, "Forgive my husband for his crassness, Mr. Whitaker." To Kane she said, "I told you of Mr. Whitaker's loss, remember?" Once again focusing on Hayward, she added, "He never listens to me, unfortunately. We were very sorry indeed to hear about your wife." Susannah didn't have to fake the remorse in her voice, it was genuine. She did feel Elsbeth's loss deeply, apparently more deeply than her own husband did. Is that why she'd committed suicide? Because her husband was fooling around with another woman?

*No man is worth it, Elsbeth.* Susannah conveyed the message silently. In response she got the feeling that she was still cold, that she hadn't even come close to solving the mystery yet. Meaning what? That Elsbeth hadn't committed suicide, after all?

"You still haven't told me where you got that necklace of yours," Hayward said. "As I told you, it is a very unique design and it was of some special consequence to my wife. In fact, it was her last wish that she be buried in it." The words were clipped, as if they'd slipped out unintentionally.

Susannah got goose bumps. Elsbeth had been *buried* wearing this necklace? Well, not this exact one, but the twin of Susannah's great-grandmother's. Elsbeth's ghost must have recognized the necklace! That's why she'd chosen Susannah to help her. "Would the dear friend of your poor departed wife to whom you referred earlier by chance be Mrs. Hall?" Susannah asked. She could see by the look in Hayward's eyes that it was. "Because I'm very close to Althea Hall." That much was true; after all, the woman *had* been her great-grandmother. "I admired the design and had a copy made."

The man still looked suspicious. "The design was done especially for Elsbeth and her friend. The jeweler was supposed to destroy the mold."

"I know that. Mrs. Hall and I shared the same jeweler. And as a favor to me, the jeweler made another necklace before destroying the mold, providing that I promised not to tell anyone. And here I am, spilling the beans."

"Spilling the beans?"

"Just an expression," she hurriedly replied.

"And your name is?" Hayward demanded.

"Again I must apologize. I don't know what's happened to my manners. My name is Susannah Ha—" A discreet jab from Kane reminded her. "Wilder. Mrs. Susannah Wilder and this is my husband, Kane. We've come from a long distance away to offer our condolences." And to find out what really happened with your wife's suicide, she silently added.

"I must say your manner is most peculiar. You use expressions I'm not familiar with and there is something about your conduct that is most out of the ordinary. Where exactly are you from?" Hayward asked.

"We're from France," Kane heard himself say. "That's why we're different," he tacked on.

"France?" Hayward repeated.

Susannah could identify with Hayward's incredulity, as she felt the same way herself. Where the heck had Kane come up with a comment like that?

* * *

"We're from France," Susannah mimicked once they were back on the street and away from Hayward Whitaker's office. "I can't believe you said that! Lucky for you I speak French. I knew my minor in French poetry would come in handy some day," she murmured to herself.

"I thought I covered things just fine," Kane retorted. "He bought my story about us meeting in Europe, that we were raised over there by American parents living in the French countryside."

"But you tripped up big-time by not being able to speak any French," she took pleasure in reminding him.

"I covered that by saying my heritage was Polish."

"Sounded like you made it up to me. The story *and* the Polish words."

"I'll have you know that those were honest-to-God Polish curses my granddad taught me."

"Great. Lucky for you Hayward didn't know Polish."

"If I was really *lucky,* I wouldn't be in this fix with you," Kane retorted. "So what did we learn from our little visit?"

"That he's definitely not the grieving widower."

Kane was about to reply when someone bumped into him before moving on down the busy thoroughfare. Instinctively checking for his wallet, Kane found it was gone. The thief, a kid of about nine or ten, was running off even as Kane took chase. "Hey, you, come back here!" Kane shouted.

Kane thought he was in good shape, but it was all he could do to keep up with the swift pace of the little pickpocket. He finally caught up with him a block later. Grabbing him by the back of his collar, Kane stopped the kid in his tracks.

"Give me my wallet, you little rug-rat," Kane growled, shaking the boy to prove he meant business.

It was like shaking an orange tree. Only instead of fruit, wallets and billfolds dropped out of the kid's jacket. As luck would have it, Kane's wallet opened up when it hit the sidewalk, and his charge card fell out, hologram shining in the sunlight. Swearing, Kane quickly grabbed it and his wallet, stuffing both in the inside pocket of his jacket.

The kid's eyes were as big as silver dollars.

"Listen, you little juvenile delinquent . . ." Kane began.

"Let the poor boy go, can't you see you're scaring him?" Susannah breathlessly interrupted as she finally caught up with them. Damn these long skinny skirts for making running impossible. Walking was hard enough. And the bustle contraption had to go. At least with those big hoopskirts you could lean backward and forward and get a little breeze going, or so her friend who did Civil War reenactments had told her. But the outfit she was wearing now was torture, or as close to it as she cared to get.

"Poor boy?" Kane repeated. "This kid is a thief. Look at all those wallets." Holding the kid with one hand, he reached down to grab a handful of wallets, holding them up for her perusal.

"Wait a second. You're Mikey, aren't you?" She directed her question to the young boy squirming in Kane's hold. "From the boardinghouse? Mrs. Broadstreet's, uh, helper." Susannah wasn't sure what to call him. Servant? Boy?

"An' what if I am," the young boy retorted, sticking his freckled chin out and reminding Susannah of one of the kids from the old "Our Gang" series. The boy's red hair and green eyes proclaimed his Irish heritage.

"I'm sure she wouldn't approve of your current activities," Susannah said.

"Then don't be tellin' her," the boy replied.

"Perhaps we won't if you'll do something for us. What do you know about Mr. Hayward Whitaker?"

Mikey shrugged, his shoulders ending up near his large ears as a result of the hold Kane maintained on his collar. "That he's a fancy lawyer. Word is his wife took a leap off the staircase. They say her ghost already haunts the place!"

The boy's voice lowered to a whisper with this last piece of information.

"You afraid of ghosts?" Kane asked.

"Naw," young Mikey scoffed, with a nervous look around. "'Tain't a good thing to be talkin' about the dead this way, though. Just in case."

"You know anything else about Whitaker?" Kane demanded.

"How come you want to know?" Mikey said.

"Never mind that," Kane countered.

"I don't know nothing else. But I do know who could find out for you."

"Who?"

"Mr. Ogilvie. He's the best detective in Savannah!"

"Then I doubt we can afford him," Kane muttered.

"Oh, he works cheap. I mean, he would if I was to say that you was friends of mine."

"And I suppose we'd become friends of yours by overlooking this little pickpocketing incident, hmm?" Kane inquired.

Mikey nodded. "That's right, sir."

"In your dreams, kid," Kane growled.

"Hold on a minute, here," Susannah interjected. "I think we should pay this Mr. Ogilvie a call."

"You would," Kane said. "Here, take these wallets while I get a good hold on this kid before he takes off again."

He handed over the half-dozen or so billfolds, larger than his—no doubt designed that way to accommodate the larger paper money of this time. One of the plainer billfolds opened up in Susannah's hand, displaying a small picture of Elsbeth. Seeing her, Susannah's heart went to her throat. Elsbeth appeared to be looking right at her and there was a connection so strong it made her catch her breath. *What are you trying to tell me?* she silently asked the likeness.

"Did you steal Mr. Whitaker's wallet?" Susannah demanded.

Mikey forcefully shook his head. "If'n I'd have stole his wallet, I wouldn't have needed to steal no more. His would've been thick enough all by itself for me to call it a day."

"You're calling it a day right now, and I'm calling the police," Kane stated.

"Calm down," Susannah advised Kane even as she looked through the billfold. There was a calling card in it. Gordon Stevens. "This billfold has a photo of Elsbeth in it," Susannah told Kane.

"What's a pho-to?" Mikey demanded, trying to get a look.

Susannah knew that photography was making its debut during this time period, although it did date back to the Civil War in experimental forms.

*"Regardez la cam-er-a, s'il vous plaît,"* Kane murmured with a devilish and-you-said-I-couldn't-speak-French grin.

"Knock it off," she muttered.

Mikey stared up at them, wide-eyed. "I ain't never met anyone like you two. Sir. Ma'am," he belatedly tacked on.

"And you're not likely to again," Kane noted.

"I reckon not."

"Mikey, who is this Gordon Stevens?"

"I can't be thinking when this man is choking the very life out of me," Mikey said with a dramatic gasp worthy of the stage.

"Loosen your grip," Susannah told Kane. "And let's bring Mikey over to that bench in the park across the street. We don't want to gather too much attention, standing here this way."

Muttering under his breath, Kane followed her suggestion, plunking the kid on the bench and keeping him there with a forceful hand on the young pickpocket's shoulder. "Now tell us what you know about Gordon Stevens," he ordered Mikey.

"I don't know nothing about him, 'cept that he's Old Man Whitaker's clerk or something like that."

Stevens... Susannah recalled that Hayward Whitaker had bellowed that name when looking for his clerk.

"Don't you think it's strange that this Gordon Stevens would carry the picture of his boss's dead wife around in his wallet?" Susannah murmured to Kane.

"No stranger than anything else I've seen in the past twenty-four hours," Kane countered.

"My detective friend is real good at figuring out strange stuff," Mikey said.

Susannah looked through the rest of Gordon Stevens's plain black billfold, but found nothing else. Just some money, not a lot. No other keepsakes or clues. She briefly considered returning the wallet to the law clerk, but decided that would involve too many questions being asked.

"We've got to return these wallets and do it as quickly and unobtrusively as possible," Susannah noted thoughtfully. "There's a soldier over there, he seems official looking." Actually the man's gray Confederate uniform looked a little worn around the edges, but his demeanor was authoritative. "I'll ask him how to find a policeman."

"He *is* a policeman," Mikey said. "You don't want to go talking to him. You're not from around here, are you." It wasn't a question.

"We're from France," Kane said.

"You eat frog legs?" Mikey demanded, seemingly intrigued by the idea.

"I prefer a cheeseburger," Kane replied.

"A what?"

"Never mind," Susannah interjected. "You two stay out of trouble while I turn these wallets over to the policeman." Without waiting for Kane's agreement, she made a beeline for the uniformed official. "I found these beneath that bench over there, officer," she said, pointing to a bench at the opposite side of the park from where Mikey and Kane were waiting. She tried batting her eyelashes at the officer, but her hat fell down on her forehead. When she almost poked him in the eye with her closed parasol while handing over the wallets, the policeman seemed eager to get rid of her before she did him bodily harm. So much for her Mata Hari ways, Susannah thought to herself with a grin.

Susannah wasn't sure what she was expecting Oliver Ogilvie to look like, but the reality surprised her. He was middle-aged, stocky, and fully bearded. He had bushy hair and thick eyebrows, but the accent and sharp gaze of Sherlock Holmes. She half expected him to say, "My dear Watson..."

Instead he said, "Well, then, Mikey, what have you brought me here?"

"Customers," Mikey said. "They're staying at Mrs. B.'s and they're looking for information about Whitaker."

Oliver Ogilvie raised his reddish eyebrows. "Well, now that sounds most interesting. Would it be Hayward Whitaker to whom you were referring?"

"That's the gent," Mikey replied.

"I can talk on my own behalf, kid," Kane growled irritably. Confronting Oliver, Kane said, "Did you know this little rug-rat is a pickpocket? I caught him trying to steal my wallet an hour ago."

"I didn't try, I done it. Right successful," Mikey boasted.

Oliver shook his head in displeasure. "I thought we'd agreed that you weren't going to be involving yourself in that kind of activity any longer, Michael."

The youngster squirmed.

"I can't have anyone working for me who is not trustworthy," Oliver firmly declared. "Perhaps this would be a good time for you to sweep out the storage room while you deliberate on your actions."

Mikey scuffed his feet a bit, a wave of red riding his pale cheeks before he shuffled off to the storage room.

"Is he your kid?" Kane asked Oliver after Mikey had left.

"You certainly are blunt, sir," Oliver observed. "The answer is no, he is not my son. No relation at all. But I feel sorry for the poor boy. His mother died when he was but a baby. She was working as a maid in Mrs. Broadstreet's household at the time. Good Christian woman that Mrs. Broadstreet is, she took him in and has done her best, but the boy often runs wild. I fear she'll be tempted to hand him over to an orphanage if he doesn't reform soon. I first met him much the same way you did, a year or so ago. He'd stolen my billfold. I sat him down and had a good talk with him, put him to work around here, tried to give him some guidance.''

''Doesn't seem to have done much good,'' Kane noted.

''This is the first time that he's strayed.''

''That you know about.''

''Oh, I'd know. But I doubt that you came here to talk to me about Mikey's problems. He mentioned something about the Whitakers?''

''That's right. But before we tell you anything more, I'd like some information about you. Your references, how long you've been doing this kind of work, that sort of thing.''

Oliver nodded, his bushy hair bobbing. ''Most certainly I can understand your caution. I have a file of references that you are welcome to look over.'' Getting up, he went over to a wooden file cabinet, where he removed a few papers that he handed over. Since Kane had a hard time reading the old-fashioned script, he handed them on to Susannah.

''If you're so good, why aren't you working for the Pinkerton agency?'' Susannah inquired after reading several of the letters. They were all complimentary. But there weren't many and they could have been forged, for all she knew.

''Allan Pinkerton is a good man. But I prefer to work on my own. If you'd prefer working with an agency man, I can refer you to one.''

''How much do they charge?'' Kane asked.

Oliver listed an amount that was more than they could afford.

''And how much do you charge?'' Kane asked.

"That depends on the case. I like a challenging mystery. And I am aware of the unusual circumstances surrounding Mrs. Whitaker's unfortunate death last month."

"What unusual circumstances?" Susannah wanted to know.

"The fact that it's widely rumored that she committed suicide, although the family had the death listed on the death certificate as an accident." At their questioning look, Oliver added, "I have a friend in the coroner's office."

"Is she supposed to have left a suicide note or anything like that?" Susannah asked.

Oliver shook his head. "Not that I've heard. But what is your interest in this case?"

"Call us friends of the family," Kane replied.

"Of Elsbeth's," Susannah clarified. "We found the news of her death most . . . disturbing. Something just isn't right about it."

"And so you'd like my help in investigating the matter further?" Oliver supplied.

"Yes," Susannah said.

"No," Kane said simultaneously.

Oliver nodded understandingly. "Perhaps I should give you two a few moments to discuss things amongst yourselves. I'll just go check and see how Mikey is doing with his sweeping. If you'll excuse me for a moment?"

"What do you mean, telling him he's hired?" Kane demanded, once Oliver had left them alone.

"What do you mean saying no?"

"I don't know enough about the guy to go blowing my money on him."

"It's not *your* money, it's *our* money. And, if I may remind you, we don't have an endless amount of time at our disposal to solve this mystery. I now only have fifteen days' worth of medication with me. And before you dare say another insulting word, I'll have you know that I'm taking that medication for a heart condition."

"You seem awfully young to have a heart condition."

She was angered by what she perceived to be suspicion in his voice. "I have a faulty mitral valve," she said curtly. "A lot of people have it. A few need medication to control an irregular heartbeat. I'm one of those few."

"Oh. Look, I'm sorry about that crack the other night," Kane quietly said. "I didn't know you were ill."

His apology surprised her and mitigated her earlier anger. "I'm not ill, per se. The thing is, I can't go off the medication. So we've got to get this mystery solved as quickly as possible. Besides, neither one of us wants to be stuck together in this situation of having to pretend to be husband and wife any longer than necessary, right?"

"Right. I'm just not convinced that hiring this detective is going to help us solve the mystery any sooner."

"I have a good feeling about him," Susannah said.

Kane groaned. "Not with the feelings again, please. I think we should sleep on it and make our decision in the morning. One more day won't hurt."

So when Oliver returned, with Mikey at his side, Kane told him, "We'll get back to you."

"By tomorrow," Susannah added.

"Are you going to go to the authorities about Mikey?" Oliver asked.

"I should," Kane replied. Seeing the defiant look in the kid's eyes, Kane took him aside and had a brief private conversation with him. After all, Kane remembered having to keep his own brother on the straight and narrow when they'd been kids. He knew how to play his cards just right, not using threats but using subtle intimidation. It had worked on Chuck and it would work on Mikey, too. "You want to be a detective like Oliver over there?" The kid nodded. "Well, you keep stealing wallets and you're gonna end up in jail yourself, not putting other people there," Kane said.

"I was just trying to help Mrs. B.," Mikey maintained with a sniff, rubbing his runny nose with his bare arm.

"You mean Mrs. Broadstreet?"

Mikey nodded. "She's a good lady. She could use the extra money."

"She's getting money from us for our room and board."

"She can always use more."

Kane sighed. He knew what it was like to be short of money when you were young. "Look, let the adults worry about Mrs. Broadstreet. She wouldn't approve of you stealing wallets to help her out."

"If you don't tell her 'bout this, I won't tell her 'bout that magical card in your wallet," Mikey said.

Kane frowned. Damn. The kid was fast. A born con artist. "That card can tell if you mess up," Kane growled.

"Mess up? I haven't messed since I was a baby," Mikey said indignantly.

"I meant I'll know if you've done anything wrong, so don't try anything. Deal?"

Mikey nodded. Spitting on his hand, he held it out to Kane. "Deal."

Grimacing, Kane shook the urchin's hand.

"You were very good with Mikey back there," Susannah noted as they walked back toward their boardinghouse. Mikey had stayed behind to help Oliver.

"The kid is a rug-rat," Kane muttered.

"You were still good with him."

Kane shrugged, clearly uncomfortable with her words of praise. "That detective and the kid could be in on some kind of scheme together. Or Whitaker might have planted the kid outside his office to steal my wallet as a way of finding out who we are."

Somehow, Susannah couldn't see Mikey working for Hayward Whitaker. Besides, there wasn't time for that kind of plan to have been set up ahead of time. "You don't trust anyone, do you?"

"Not many people, no. And certainly not those I've just met."

His words made her stomach drop like a stone for some reason. She already knew he wasn't likely to trust her—not when his beloved kid brother swore he was having an affair with her.

"Being cautious has made me a successful business-man," Kane was saying.

"Successful, but lonely."

"What makes you think that?"

"Your attitude."

"What's wrong with my attitude?"

"You have five years or so for me to go into detail?" she mockingly inquired.

"Time is something I appear to have too much of," he drawled.

"I can tell you what I have too much of. This stupid bustle," she muttered. "I can't wait to get back to the board-inghouse and take this thing off," she added under her breath.

Kane heard her, and her words created a mental image that left him hot and bothered. He could still remember her shadowy striptease behind the dressing screen last night... the thrust of her full breasts as she reached over her head to put on her nightgown, the inward dip of her waist, the outward curve of her hips.

"They'd probably have me arrested for indecent exposure if I were to take off my jacket," she said.

Kane nodded, knowing damn well his own thoughts were indecent and inappropriate. Fate must have a strange sense of humor to have trapped him in time with the one woman who would create the most havoc in his well-ordered life.

Sighing at his silence, Susannah reached into her purse and grabbed the fan she'd gotten in her own century. Too bad she hadn't brought a battery-operated hand fan along, she was thinking. But that would have been sure to arouse suspicions and Hayward Whitaker was suspicious enough as it was. And nervous. Almost guilty, in fact. Because his wife had committed suicide on his account?

Again Susannah felt that overwhelming sense of denial whenever she thought of Elsbeth committing suicide. It was a feeling that kept getting stronger, almost as if it were being directed by Elsbeth herself.

"Can't you just come out and give me a few clues yourself?" Susannah muttered.

"Clues about what?" Kane asked.

"Nothing. I was just talking to myself." Actually she'd been talking to Elsbeth, but she wasn't about to admit that to Kane. After all, he didn't believe in ghosts.

But Susannah did. She hadn't before, but she did after seeing Elsbeth in that blue light. They'd been brought back in time too late to save Elsbeth from death. The only other logical reason would be to clear her name. She remembered thinking as much last night; and then, as now, she felt a sense of conviction. Almost as if Elsbeth were telling her, *Yes, yes yes!* Clearing Elsbeth's name because she *hadn't* committed suicide, after all?

*Bingo* was the silent response.

Susannah felt an overwhelming need to sit down.

"You don't look too well," Kane noted, leading her to a bench at the same park where they'd talked to Mikey earlier. He chose an area where a tree provided some welcome shade from the strong sunshine. "What's wrong?"

Since the bustle stuck out so far behind, Susannah had to cautiously sit sideways, almost as if she were riding sidesaddle. She needed to tell him her thoughts about Elsbeth's death. "Bear with me a minute here," Susannah told Kane. "What if Elsbeth didn't fall down those stairs, after all? What if her death wasn't a suicide?"

"You mean it could have been an accident, just as they put on the death certificate?"

Susannah paused before shaking her head. "I don't think so. What if she was pushed down those stairs?"

"By whom?"

"That's what we're here to find out," Susannah declared with conviction. "That's why she brought us back. To solve the mystery of her death."

"There's no mystery. Her husband was fooling around on her, so she threw herself down the stairs. It's criminal that some women can be so unfeeling as to take up with a married man, but it happens." Kane gave Susannah a look, reminding her that he thought she'd taken up with his married brother.

"You're way off base," she angrily retorted. "About Elsbeth *and* about me." Carefully standing, her spine as straight as the nearby oak tree, she stormed off. Well, actually, it was hard to storm when you had to take baby steps in the stupid tight skirt she was wearing. But the anger emanating from her was clear.

Kane could feel it even though he was several feet away. Susannah was a fiery woman, not one to hide her emotions. The more time he spent with her, the less he felt he knew her. And the more he wanted her.

Nothing was going according to plan. He frowned at the memory of how confidentially he'd told his sister-in-law that he had everything under control.... Had that only been less than twenty-four hours ago? Yes. But more than a hundred years in the future.

While Kane was a maverick, accustomed to being on his own and not conforming to the rules, that didn't mean he was into the concept of time travel. He prided himself on being logical and reality based. He'd never been one to be interested in things paranormal. He'd never been interested in fiery women with dark hair that curled with a life of its own, either.

That was starting to change. And he didn't like it. He had to keep his wits about him, focus on getting back to his own time period. As Susannah had so mockingly pointed out to him last night, he'd gotten used to relying on technology for the answers.

Kane doubted that even the most advanced supercomputer would be able to make sense of his relationship with Susannah, however.

Susannah wasn't able to maintain her half-block advantage over Kane for very long, but it had given her a much-needed break from his company. The problem was that she'd unintentionally lowered her defenses with him, allowed herself to like certain things about him. She'd even opened up and told him about her heart condition, for crying out loud. She rarely told anyone about that. And he'd responded with an apology—a rare occurrence for him, she was sure.

When Kane took hold of her arm, she glanced over her shoulder to give him a frosty look. Then her glance went past him and took in the words written on the storefront they were standing in front of.

His words went right over her head. Until he angrily said, "Are you listening to me?"

"No," she readily admitted. "Give me half your money."

He blinked at her. "Wha-at?"

"You heard me. I'm going to go get a soda."

"There's no way a soda can cost that much money."

"I don't like being dependent on anyone else for money. Half of that cash is mine!"

"That's not how they feel about things these days," Kane countered. "I'll buy you a soda."

"No way. I'll buy it for myself," she said stubbornly, the look in her brown eyes daring him to contradict her.

"Fine. Here." He pulled out several coins and bills and handed them to her. It wasn't half of what he had by any means, but it was enough to keep her quiet. Or so he hoped.

Susannah took the money and stashed it in her purse before regally pivoting on her heel, rather pleased she'd managed the maneuver without tripping. She was also pleased she'd stood her ground, not letting Kane walk all over her.

As she strolled into the store, she couldn't begin to identify all the intriguing aromas inside, although eucalyptus and turpentine came to mind. So did citrus.

The shelves behind the counter were filled with every kind of glass bottle imaginable, the old-fashioned kind with cork stoppers. On the walls were metal signs—a diamond-shaped one said Celery Cures Constipation while a rectangular one heralded Laxative Bromo Quinine for Colds while another praised Henderson's Digestive Tablets. A glass case was filled with more curatives, bottles and tins than you could shake a stick at.

When Susannah saw the man in the white coat, she wondered if he'd come to take her away. It was a little much to take in all at once. This looked nothing like her idea of a drugstore. But nothing was going to distract her from getting what she'd come in for. On a hot day, there was nothing she liked better than a huge lemon soda. Of course, she was used to ordering hers at Bo's Dog Stand on Forty-second Street, but this would do just fine.

"I'd like a lemon soda, please," Susannah said, licking her lips in anticipation.

Beneath the soda-fountain spigot was a sign that said Phoenix, For Your Nerves. Susannah could definitely use something for her nerves, because Kane was certainly getting on hers. The man had an absolute knack for doing that.

The soda was stronger than she was used to, but it was wonderfully refreshing as she sat on a wrought-iron chair—perched came closer to the truth, actually, due to the damn bustle. But she refused to let that distract her from the pleasure of closing her eyes in ecstasy and sipping her lemon soda.

Kane was watching her. She sensed that. He was making some purchases of his own—tooth powder, toothbrush, shaving soap, and a straight-edged razor.

"Do you need anything?" he called out.

Keeping her eyes closed, she shook her head. She had her lemon soda. That's all she needed. Not a man with blue eyes and a rare smile that creased his face with sexy appeal. She didn't need him at all. But it appeared, for the time being at least, that she was stuck with him.

As they got ready for bed that night, Kane was saying, "If you want anything done right, you've got to do it yourself or pay for the best in the business. Since we don't have the money for the latter, we'll have to do the former."

Behind the dressing screen, Susannah was discreetly finishing the last of her candy bars before swallowing her heart medication. "What about Oliver Ogilvie?"

"Did he look like the best in the business to you?"

She paused. "All right, I'll admit he's something of a character."

"That's putting it mildly."

"But I have a feeling about him," she continued as she came back into the room, dressed in her borrowed nightgown.

"Don't tell me about your feelings. That's how we got into trouble in the first place."

"No, it isn't."

"You had a feeling you had to go snooping around in that third-floor room—"

"I wasn't snooping!" she interrupted him to deny.

"And I was fool enough to come after you."

"As I've told you before, no one held a gun to your head."

"No, but they might if we get too close in this investigation. If Elsbeth really *was* murdered, then whoever did it is out there and they're not gonna be real happy about us digging around. Personally, I think the other woman did it, the redheaded one in Whitaker's office."

"Excuse me? Where did you get an outlandish idea like that from?"

"Male intuition," he drawled mockingly. "She looked the type."

"You've got the intuition of a computer chip," Susannah retorted. "And the emotions of a hard drive!"

"I'll tell you what is hard—"

She cut him off. "Don't be crude."

"Crude? To hear you talk, you'd think you were a proper uptight Victorian lady. But we both know you're not, don't we?" Kane put his hands on her shoulders, his grip firm and tempting. "We both know that you're not proper at all." Slowly drawing her to him, he huskily whispered, "You kiss like a hot Savannah night, all moist heat and pure passion."

Susannah figured there were two ways of shutting him up—hitting him or kissing him. She opted for the latter.

# Six

Susannah was delighted at the astonishment she tasted on Kane's lips. She felt a surprising sense of feminine power wash over her. Every other time, Kane had kissed *her* senseless. Not this time. This time would be different, she silently vowed. She'd scramble *his* brains, for a change. Make *him* all hot and bothered. And she'd come out of the encounter cool, calm and collected.

But it was difficult to be any of those things when she was dressed in a thin nightgown and she could feel the heat of his body beckoning her closer. The power she'd felt before was being rapidly overcome by the sheer pleasure kissing him gave her. Feeling control slipping away from her, she forced herself to pull away.

"But enough of this fooling around," she said in a collected voice that did her self-confidence good. Inside she felt anything but cool and calm, but she had no intention of letting *him* know that. "We were supposed to be deciding whether or not to hire Mr. Ogilvie as a detective."

Kane stared at her as if he couldn't believe what he was hearing.

"Just like that?" he growled. "You can switch off just like that? And you expect me to do the same?"

The look on his face made her doubt the wisdom of her decision to rile him. Belatedly she recalled the dangers of twitching the tiger's tail.

"It's not that easy," he warned her in a dangerously soft voice.

"I realize that hiring a detective is a serious matter," she began, deliberately misunderstanding him.

"That's not what I mean and you know it."

So she confronted him. "Do you believe me when I say that I am not having an affair with your brother?"

His silence was answer enough.

"I didn't think so." But she had thought—or at least *hoped*. A stupid mistake.

"That being the case, we'd do best to keep any personal involvement to a minimum," she stated.

"You were the one who kissed me," Kane reminded.

"To teach you a lesson."

"That you kiss like a seductress? I already knew that."

She blinked. A seductress? Her? With her too-large thighs and wild hair? Was he making fun of her? She stared at him, but saw hunger rather than derision in his blue eyes.

Apparently Kane was as attracted to her as she was to him. And as unhappy about it. It was a startling discovery. Kind of like finding out that keg you were sitting on was filled with dynamite.

"Uh..." She looked away, scrambling to get her thoughts in order. "Um, I think we should hire Mr. Ogilvie to help us. He knows more about the ins and outs of Savannah society than we have time to find out."

"Did you ever consider the fact that Whitaker might contact your great-grandmother to see if your story checks out?" Kane suddenly asked.

Susannah's heart dropped. She hadn't thought of that. "Maybe we should go see my great-grandmother ourselves and tell her that her friend didn't commit suicide, she was murdered."

"Oh, right," Kane scoffed. "You think your great-grandmother is going to believe you if you show up on her doorstep claiming to be her great-granddaughter from over one hundred years in the future— 'Oh, and by the way, your best friend was murdered'? Dream on."

"There's no need to get nasty about it."

"You haven't seen 'nasty.'"

"I certainly have," she told him. "You were incredibly nasty when you accosted me at the convention center."

"Accosted?"

"You know what I mean. And one day you're going to apologize for your behavior," she vowed.

"That's about as likely as—"

"As a ghost leading you back a century to solve her murder?" she countered.

To her surprise, he smiled. "Yeah, it's about as likely as that. Okay, we'll hire this Ogilvie guy and see what he comes up with. You want me to turn out the light?"

Susannah nodded. "Please."


Susannah woke the next morning to the sound of curses— Polish curses? Opening her eyes, she peered through the white mosquito netting to see Kane standing at the chest of drawers, leaning forward toward the mirror. He was wearing pants but no shirt. Without benefit of the suspenders, the pants hung low on his hips, providing a tantalizing glimpse of the small of his back. He had a great tush.

He swore again.

Shoving the netting and her sexy thoughts aside, she climbed out of bed and asked, "What are you doing?"

He turned, a straight razor in his right hand.

"Oh, I see," she murmured, noting the tiny nicks on his face. "Trying to commit hara-kiri, are you?"

"You think you can do any better, you're welcome to try," he retorted without thinking.

Her eyebrows lifted. "You mean you're actually willing to trust me with a sharp weapon in my hand?"

"On second thought," he said, turning back to the mirror, "I'll do it myself."

Susannah had to admit that the idea of having him at her mercy did have its appeal. So did the idea of smoothing her fingers over the contours of his face, feeling the rasp of his skin beneath her fingertips. She closed her eyes and pictured herself shaving him, with him seated before her, his head resting against her—just beneath her breasts—as she gently moved the razor over his lathered face. The mental image was enough to raise her body temperature and make her pull at the neckline of her nightgown in a futile attempt to get some air.

"Something wrong?" Kane asked her.

Her eyes flew open as she shook her head. "No, nothing. The sight of blood just leaves me feeling a bit weak."

Actually it was the sight of a half-dressed Kane that left her feeling weak!

"They don't even have toilet paper I can use on the damn cuts," Kane was grumbling as he finished getting dressed.

His grumbling snapped her out of her reverie and sent her in search of her purse. She removed a small packet of tissues and handed him one. "Here, this should help. Do you think you should use antiseptic on it?"

"Don't tell me you've got that in your bag, as well?"

"I like to travel prepared."

"Prepared for what?"

"Every eventuality."

"Including century hopping?"

She grinned. "If necessary. Although if I'd known I'd be landing in the 1880s, I'd have brought along a few more necessities, like clothes. And my feather bed."

"A dozen pairs of Jockey shorts, jeans and some denim shirts," Kane interjected. "And my notebook computer."

"Feeling lost without it, are you?" she teased him.

"You could say that."

They shared a look of such camaraderie that Kane got spooked. What had happened to the hostility between them? The only way he could keep his distance from Susannah was to think of her as the seductive "other woman" who'd broken up his kid brother's marriage.

What if she is telling the truth? a nagging little voice inside Kane's head demanded. What if she isn't involved with Chuck? It still meant his brother had a crush on her. An even better question might have been, What would have happened if I'd met her first? Kane thought to himself. What if she'd never met Chuck and we didn't have that baggage to deal with? What would I do then?

He knew. He'd make her his. The discovery hit him like a lightning bolt.

"You okay?" Susannah asked him, seeing what could only be described as a flabbergasted expression on his face.

"Yeah," he muttered. "I'll wait for you downstairs."

He was gone before she could say a word. Mrs. Broadstreet had left the trunk she'd had brought down from the attic in their room. Susannah went through it now, and selected a skirt in a lovely shade of yellow. She had no problem putting on the matching top, which didn't need a chemise beneath it because the material was thick enough on its own.

*Another morning, another fashion challenge,* Susannah thought to herself as she struggled to get dressed. She didn't get very far. Oh, she got the top on okay. But then she got stuck fastening the petticoat ties on the waistband of the hoop underskirt—crinoline, she corrected herself. Since she was alone into the room, she hadn't gone behind the dressing screen.

And so it was that Kane found her standing there in her bikini underwear and hoop underskirt when he walked back into the room a few seconds later. She almost shrieked as she looked over her shoulder to find him standing there.

"You look like an X-rated Bo-Peep," Kane said, his drawl as ravishing as his gaze, which settled on her with the sensual energy of a touch.

Disconcerted, Susannah grabbed the coverlet from the bed to cover herself with. "What are you doing back up here?"

"I was going to ask you if you wanted me to bring Mrs. Broadstreet up to help you out."

"No. You'll have to help me. I can't get this bow tied around my waist," she muttered in frustration. "Mrs. Broadstreet can't see me this way—she'd be shocked to see me in this kind of underwear."

Susannah noted that Kane didn't appear to be shocked by her appearance. Instead, he seemed downright pleased about it. And he sure seemed to be taking his time tying a bow in the back. Suspicious, she impatiently demanded, "Is there a problem?"

Only with his blood flow, Kane thought to himself. It seemed to have all gathered below his belt—due to the seductive view he had of her luscious backside, where the coverlet didn't cover her at all. The hoopskirt contraption was skeletal and allowed him an unobstructed view of her lower torso. Susannah had long legs. She wasn't skinny. She was curved and soft.

"Is there a problem?" Susannah irritably repeated, turning her head until her chin rested on her right shoulder as she tried to see what he was doing back there.

"No, no problem," Kane muttered, all thumbs as he tried for the fifth time to tie a bow. "There. That will have to do."

"While you're here you might as well help me get the skirt on over this thing," Susannah said, her tone of voice efficient and practical. Unlike her nervous system, which was humming with awareness.

Together they managed to get her skirt on with less trouble than they'd had with the bow. Perhaps that was because Kane was suddenly in as much of a hurry to get her covered up as she was. His fingers shook just remembering the way she'd looked when he'd walked into the room. His pants, which had been loose-fitting before, were fast becoming snug and uncomfortable as a result of his steamy thoughts.

"Ready?" she asked him.

Hell, he was ready, all right! Ready to seduce her there and then. But he wasn't sure who would truly be the seduced and who would be the seducer. And he still wasn't sure that she wasn't responsible for almost breaking up his brother's marriage. He only knew she was responsible for making him as hard as the damn straw mattress they slept on. Together. All night long. Kane groaned. It was going to be a *long* day. And an even longer night!

As Susannah carefully made her way downstairs, she paused at the bottom of the stairs to study her surroundings. Yesterday, she'd been too wound up to notice much about the house. She did remember that the dining room was on the right, and the front parlor on the left.

Pausing, she took a quick peek into the parlor. The huge room was stuffed full from fanlight to floor with settees, divans, armchairs and several ornate tables, on which were placed a collection of knickknacks. Pastoral paintings and prints hung by long cords well above *and* below eye level. The mantel above the fireplace was filled from end to end with vases of every size, color and shape. In the far corner, beside a piano covered with a colorful silk shawl, was a collection of fans, opened to display their artistry. Near the velvet-draped doorway, peacock feathers were displayed in a huge Chinese ginger jar while a china cabinet against the far wall was chockablock filled with porcelain figurines. It was all a little mind-boggling.

Dusting the room must take a week, Susannah thought to herself.

By comparison, the dining room was almost empty, aside from the large dining table and a ponderous sideboard with its intricately carved ornamental backpiece. The top was marble and cool to her fingertips as she ran them over it while she walked by. It was a way of physically reminding herself that this was indeed reality.

Reality was also catching Mikey, who was kneeling on the floor reaching into the ample cupboard below the sideboard.

"What are you doing?" Susannah asked.

He jerked like a kid caught with his hand in the cookie jar. Indeed, he did have a cookie in one hand, and a round cookie tin in the other.

"Do you sneak up on folks like that in France?" Mikey demanded, hurriedly replacing the lid and stashing the cookie tin back where it belonged.

"Is that a sugar cookie?" Susannah demanded. "Listen, I'll trade you a pile of grits for that cookie."

"You don't like grits in France?"

"I prefer cookies," Susannah admitted.

"So do I," Mikey stated, his chin pugnaciously stuck out. His hair stuck out too, in a stubborn cowlick.

Susannah sighed. "Okay, keep the cookie."

"I already tried to bribe the kid," Kane murmured in her ear. "But it was no go."

Mikey stared at them with a frown. "Is everyone from France like you?"

Susannah just grinned and shook her head.

"Now don't you be pestering our guests," Mrs. Broadstreet scolded the boy as she walked into the room. "Cook has work for you in the kitchen." Once the boy had left, she turned to apologize. "I'm sorry about that. Mikey means well. His manners need improving and no matter how I try, I don't seem to be doing a good job in that direction. Gerta, do be careful with that platter," she warned as the maid awkwardly made her way toward the sideboard. "I pride myself on running an efficient household, you know," Mrs. Broadstreet went on to tell Susannah. "I follow all the wonderful advice given in Catharine Beecher's book on housekeeping, *The American Woman's Home*. Are you familiar with it?''

''No.'' Susannah wasn't all that familiar with housekeeping, period. Or perhaps it would be more accurate to say she was familiar with it and familiarity bred contempt. She even had a magnet on her fridge that said Dull Women Have Immaculate Houses.

''The book is wonderful,'' their landlady raved. ''She is most modern in her approach.''

Susannah doubted the author was as modern as *she* was.

''She treats housekeeping as if it were a science.''

Susannah had always hated science. She hated the awkward way Kane made her feel even more. She needed some time away from him, time to get her thoughts together. ''I'd love to see your kitchen,'' Susannah told Mrs. Broadstreet.

''What about breakfast?'' Kane demanded.

''You go ahead without me,'' Susannah said. ''I'll have some bread and jam afterward.''

''What's the rush, dear?'' Kane mockingly inquired. ''The kitchen will still be there after you've eaten. After all, I wouldn't want your grits to get cold.''

''Thank you, honey pie,'' she said with enough sweetness to gag a chocoholic. ''Don't you worry about me. You just go right on and eat those grits yourself. After all, a girl has got to look out for her girlish figure.''

''I'll look out for your figure,'' Kane drawled, his gaze settling on her body as if he could see what lay beneath her multiple layers of clothing. Since he'd seen her standing half-naked shortly before, she had no doubt he was having no difficulty recalling what she looked like. The realization made her even more desperate to get away.

Linking her arm through the older woman's, Susannah said, ''Come, Mrs. B. You don't mind if I call you Mrs. B. the way Mikey does, do you? Let's go into the kitchen and dish the dirt.''

''Dirt? There's no dirt in my kitchen!'' Mrs. B. denied in an affronted voice before pulling away from Susannah.

"I'm sorry," she swiftly apologized. "I certainly didn't mean to imply.., That is...it's just an expression, meaning to talk and gossip."

"You do use the strangest expressions. Mikey told me you're from France. My husband and I went to Europe on our honeymoon. We visited Paris at that time and I must say that we didn't meet anyone who paints their nails and talks in such a strange manner."

"Oh, Kane and I are unique, I'll grant you that," Susannah breezily declared. Kane had her so rattled this morning, she wasn't thinking straight.

"I don't paint my nails, though," Kane said dryly.

"Very funny," Susannah snapped.

"I live to amuse you, honey pie," he replied with a devilish grin.

He lived to irritate her, Susannah thought to herself. And he was doing much too good a job of it.

Mrs. B. gave them both an uneasy look. "If you'd like to speak to me alone, we could take tea in the front parlor."

"That would be lovely," Susannah said.

"It's not that I have anything to hide in the kitchen," Mrs. B. hurriedly assured her. "It's just that Cook does tend to be a little testy if a stranger comes into her kitchen. I could arrange for you to visit some other time, perhaps."

"That would be fine. We'll be in the parlor," Susannah told Kane.

"Bring us tea on the tea cart, Gerta," Mrs. B. said.

"Is not teatime now," Gerta said with a confused look.

"That's all right. We'll make it a special occasion."

Mrs. B. didn't relax until Gerta had pushed the tea cart into the parlor and left. "The girl is trying her best, I know, but I fear I won't have a breakable item left in the household."

Noticing all the bric-a-brac in this room alone, Susannah doubted that.

"The weather appears to be most agreeable today," Mrs. B. said.

Susannah nodded. "You've got a lovely parlor here." Which was true. Although crowded, it *was* lovely. "And some very nice paintings, as well."

"Thank you. My husband fancied himself to be something of a collector. He collected etchings of horses. We have them all over the house. The chromolithographs are those selected by Catharine Beecher for their refinement in taste." Mrs. B. nodded to one print Susannah recognized as Bierstadt's *Sunset in the Yosemite Valley.* "She talks about it in her book. Would you care for sugar?"

Susannah nodded. "Thank you. I apologize for the misunderstanding earlier," she added, before taking the delicate teacup and saucer handed to her. "I wouldn't want you thinking that I have no manners at all. It's just that I'm not used to all the social mores in this part of the world yet."

"'Elegant manners will carry a stranger further up the heights of social ambition than money, personal beauty, or mental culture.' I read that in one of my social etiquette books," Mrs. B. confided.

"Maybe you should lend me one," Susannah suggested.

"Certainly. I keep them on the shelf right here." She got up and walked the few steps to the bookcase. Setting down her teacup, Susannah followed suit. "You're more than welcome to borrow any volume that appeals to you."

After some consideration, she selected *The American Code of Manners.*

Mrs. B. was much too well mannered to directly inquire why Susannah had wanted to speak to her in private. And Susannah knew she couldn't just jump in and ask their landlady if she knew anything about Elsbeth Whitaker; she'd learned that much about the social etiquette of the times.

So she let Mrs. B. set the pace, listening to her talk about Savannah and how it had changed over the years. "There are many in society here who haven't forgiven me for marrying a Northerner after the war between the states."

"You mean the Civil War?"

"There was nothing *civil* about it."

"I imagine not." Susannah knew how devastating the war had been.

"When I married, I was slighted by society. After my husband died, I realized boarding offered a good chance to make money and not lose social class. I had already lost so much of my position here, I didn't want to slip even further. During that time, Elsbeth Whitaker was one of the few who was kind to me."

"You knew Elsbeth Whitaker?"

"Not well. She was younger than I. Hers is such a tragic story, really. She came from a very old family here in Savannah. Her family arranged her marriage to Hayward Whitaker, whose family lines go all the way back to those of the state's first settlers, right along with General Oglethorpe, who founded Savannah. The couple had two children, but both died in their infancy. And then Elsbeth herself died just this past month. Sad story indeed." Before Susannah could comment, Mrs. B. went on to more social gossip, none of which was relevant to Elsbeth. Knowing she couldn't rush her, Susannah listened politely as the older woman began practicing her schoolgirl French.

Reverting to English, Mrs. B. reminisced, "I did so enjoy our time in Paris while on my honeymoon. Are you from that lovely city?"

Susannah shook her head, hating to lie, but knowing there was no way she could tell the truth. "I grew up in the countryside." It was true—just the Connecticut countryside, not the French countryside.

"Perhaps I've visited your hometown?"

"I don't think so," Susannah replied, thinking of the twentieth-century suburb where she'd grown up. "Tell me more about Elsbeth Whitaker," she prompted, her patience nearing an end.

"There's not much more to tell. Her death was a great tragedy."

Susannah couldn't help herself. She had to ask. She tried to be as discreet as possible. "Do you know if there was any mention of any romantic indiscretions attached to Mr. Whitaker's name?"

"I'm sure I don't know. And even if I did, it wouldn't do to talk about it with strangers."

Susannah sighed, ruefully acknowledging that in Mrs. B.'s eyes, people probably didn't come much stranger than herself and Kane.

"I appreciate your discretion," Susannah murmured, thinking once again that it was a good thing they were hiring Mr. Ogilvie this morning. Because she and Kane were bound to get bogged down in sticky social testiness, were they to try gathering too much information on their own. That didn't mean she was going to sit around and twiddle her thumbs, however.

In fact, Susannah had a plan up her sleeve for doing a little additional investigative work on her own later that very afternoon.

"We'd like to hire you, Mr. Ogilvie," Susannah said.

"I'm glad to hear that," Oliver Ogilvie replied. "I confess, I've done a little preliminary research on my own. I had a feeling you might be returning."

Susannah couldn't resist giving Kane a triumphant look, one that said, See, I'm not the only one who has feelings about things.

"And please do call me Oliver," the detective added.

"How about starting off by telling us who the redheaded woman was in Whitaker's office yesterday. The two of them looked to be more than just good friends," Kane said.

"She had a dark beauty mark near her mouth." Susannah almost added, *Like Cindy Crawford,* but stopped herself in time. "And she was wearing tea-rose perfume. I haven't smelled anything else like it since I've been here."

"That sounds like Mrs. Lucille Hilton," Oliver Ogilvie noted. "She has a beauty mark such as you've described and her own perfume is made up especially for her. I do believe the tea rose used is even named after her.''

"Who is Mrs. Hilton?"

"She's one of this city's leading women of beauty and a client of Hayward Whitaker's.''

"They looked to be more than just attorney and client," Susannah noted. "Where was Hayward Whitaker the night Elsbeth died?''

"He spent the evening at home.''

"Where was Mrs. Hilton?" Kane demanded.

"She was visiting Mr. Whitaker regarding a legal matter of some kind concerning her recently deceased husband.''

"Wait a second, here. You mean she knocked off her old man, too?" Kane exclaimed.

Oliver blinked in surprise. "Excuse me?''

"Sweetums, you're confusing Oliver with your strange language," Susannah sweetly warned Kane.

"Thank you for pointing that out to me, sweetie pie," Kane retorted, putting an arm around her waist and squeezing. "Forgive the display of affection, Oliver, but we haven't been together all that long.''

As in two days, Susannah silently supplied. Already it felt like two lifetimes!

"Newlyweds, eh?" Oliver inquired with a grin and a wiggle of his bushy, brick red eyebrows.

"Something like that," Susannah murmured.

"I don't suppose Mrs. Hilton knocked off—I mean, killed her husband . . . by pushing him down the stairs, did she?" Kane asked, ignoring Susannah's glare as she stepped away from him.

"No," Oliver replied. "His heart gave out.''

"Helped along by his blushing bride, perhaps," Kane said.

"You have reason to suspect Mrs. Hilton of killing her husband? The man was eighty and in poor health.''

"And she looks to be much younger than that and in fine health.''

"I'll certainly make some inquiries," Oliver said, scribbling down some notes on a sheet of paper.

Susannah could actually hear the scratchy sound the pen's nib made as it went over the paper. Seeing her interest, Oliver said, "It's a new contraption, manufactured by Lewis Waterman. First practical hydraulic or fountain pen that actually has an ink reservoir. Clever, eh?"

She nodded.

"Are you interested in new technology?" Kane inquired.

"Most definitely. But I digress. I will check further into Mrs. Hilton's possible involvement."

"I don't think she did it," Susannah said. "I'd keep checking Hayward's exact whereabouts in the house that night."

"I have a contact that can speak to the servants in the house. Perhaps they will come up with additional details," Oliver replied.

Once Susannah and Kane were outside, Kane made the sudden announcement, "I'm going to do a little nosing around at the tavern we were at the other night, see if I can come up with anything there."

"Don't do any more gambling," she warned him.

"What, no warnings about staying away from your pal Polly?" he mocked.

"You don't seem to pay much attention to what I say, so why should I bother giving you advice?" Rather pleased to have had the last word, she walked up the steps to the front door of the boardinghouse. Discreetly looking over her shoulder, she waited until Kane was out of sight before turning around and going back down the steps.

"You going somewhere?" Mikey asked from the sidewalk.

Startled, she demanded, "How long have you been standing there?"

"Long enough to see you pretend to go inside."

"I was not pretending. I merely changed my mind." Now that she thought about it, Mikey's presence could add some much-needed respectability to her plans.

"I've got a job for you, Mikey," she began.

"I'm not stealing wallets anymore," the lad declared.

"Not that kind of job. I'd like you to accompany me while I... while I go shopping," she fabricated.

"Shopping?" Mikey's face had the same distrustful look any male got when that word was mentioned.

"That's right. Everyone knows that when the going gets tough, the tough go shopping," she told the boy. "I'll pay you three cents if you'll come along to hold my purchases once I make them. Deal?" She didn't know if that was a generous amount or not in 1884's economy, but apparently it was good enough for Mikey.

Seeing that he was about to spit in his palm the way he had at Oliver's office the day before, Susannah hurriedly said, "There's no need for that. Here." She dug around in the clear plastic bag she had placed the nineteenth-century money in, taking out the coins one by one. They looked nothing like pennies of her own time. Instead of a portrait of Lincoln, these had a seated woman on them.

After quickly pocketing the coins, Mikey accompanied her, all the time saying, "There aren't no shops this way."

"I know where I'm going," Susannah maintained. "We'll just stop at Mr. Whitaker's law office while we're out."

"You gonna tell him about me stealing wallets?" Mikey demanded, thrusting his pugnacious jaw out. The freckles on his nose fairly danced with annoyance.

"No. My business is... personal."

Unlike her last visit, this time there was a man—blond, with the face of an angel—seated at the desk outside Mr. Whitaker's office. When he turned his head she saw that on the far side of his left cheek were deep scars—smallpox scars—marring his otherwise-perfect countenance. In keeping with the fashion of the day—when facial hair indicated masculinity and virility—he had a mustache and side-burns.

"Mr. Whitaker isn't in," Gordon Stevens told her. The law clerk was younger than Susannah expected. For an eerie moment, he rather reminded her of Kane's brother Charles, or Chuck, as he called him.

"I didn't wish to speak to Mr. Whitaker. I merely stopped by to inquire if I'd left my handkerchief behind yesterday." God, I sound like Scarlett O'Hara, Susannah thought.

"I don't believe we've found a handkerchief," Stevens said.

Susannah fiddled with her necklace as she said, "Well, fiddle-de-dee. You're sure? It had lace at the edges and little embroidered flowers on it." Then, as Gordon Stevens's eyes fastened on her garnet necklace just as she'd intended, she exclaimed, "Why, Mr. Stevens, I must say that I find your interest in my necklace to be most ungentlemanly."

The law clerk blushed and stammered an apology. "It's just that your necklace reminds me of—"

"Elsbeth Whitaker? I've heard. Such a tragic story. Mr. Whitaker told me that she was buried wearing this necklace, or one that looks just like it. Can you imagine?"

The law clerk's face went from red to white.

"Poor boy, I've upset you." *Why is that?* Susannah thought to herself, her instincts on red alert again. *Do you know something about Elsbeth's death, Gordon? Are you hiding some secret about your boss's involvement?*

"I have a lot of work to get done before Mr. Whitaker returns," the law clerk said. "I'm sorry I wasn't able to help you find your handkerchief."

*Oh, I found what I was looking for, all right,* Susannah thought. "Why, don't you worry about a thing. I'll just speak to Mr. Whitaker when he gets home this evening."

"He's got an important meeting this evening."

"Then I'll stop by here to see him."

"The meeting isn't here."

"Oh?" Susannah let the silence hang in the air, waiting for it to force Stevens into saying something.

Other than fidgeting with the papers on his desk, he made no further comment about his boss's plans for the evening. Instead he repeated, a bit more desperately this time, "I must get back to work. I have a great deal to do."

So do I, Susannah thought to herself.

When Susannah returned to her room at the boarding-house, she found that Kane still hadn't come back. The un-expected bit of privacy was welcome. Warm after her long walk, she peeled off her outer clothing and stepped out of the crinoline petticoat. While it had proved to be cooler than the tight, bustled dresses that were more fashionable now, she still longed for a pair of shorts and a tank top— Wait a second! An idea hit her.

Five minutes later, she stood in her camisole and a pair of bloomers pushed up above her knees. "Not exactly shorts, but they'll do," she murmured to herself.

She felt like celebrating her discovery that Whitaker had an important and apparently somewhat secret meeting to-night. But she'd already eaten all the chocolate bars she'd brought with her. "They would have melted otherwise," she muttered defensively, as she opened her ever-present purse. Since there were no garbage cans around, she'd worked out a system for disposing of the garbage she collected by burn-ing it in the fireplace in their room. Apparently folks in this day and age were already into recycling—papers were gath-ered together, as was just about everything else. Little went to waste.

She popped a piece of gum in her mouth and took out her portable cassette player. Putting the headphones on, she closed her eyes and pretended she was back in her own time, in her own apartment. Before long, the beat of Billy Joel's greatest-hits cassette got her to boogying around the room. Susannah turned the volume up even higher, holding an in-visible mike as she lip-synched the words to the song.

A scream shattered her concentration. It hadn't come from Billy Joel.

Opening her eyes, Susannah was horrified to see Gerta standing just inside the doorway, with a pile of clean sheets in her arms.

Gerta stared at her, bug-eyed. *"Gott im Himmel!"* she shrieked. Dropping the sheets and frantically crossing herself, the maid ran screaming from the room.

# Seven

Oh, God! Now she'd done it! Swearing under her breath, Susannah snatched the headphones off her head with one hand while turning off the portable cassette player with the other. Of course, the headphones got stuck in her wild wavy hair and she was further delayed trying to untangle herself without yanking a hunk of her hair out. Hiding the headphones and cassette player back in her purse, Susannah tugged on what she hoped was a dress—the garment wrapped around the front.

As she rushed downstairs, she prayed that the clothing she had on was sufficient to be seen outside her room. She certainly didn't want to raise any more eyebrows than she already had. She found Gerta and Mrs. B. both in the dining room. Since Mrs. B. didn't blink an eye at Susannah's appearance, she guessed she was okay in that department.

Gerta, however, was *not* okay. Standing behind Mrs. B. as if for protection, the maid was shivering and crying in her apron.

"Gerta says she saw you in your room and that you were possessed by the devil, with strange pounding noises coming out of your head but not out of your mouth," Mrs. B. related.

So much for lip-synching, Susannah hysterically noted. "I can explain," she hurriedly assured her landlady.

"I hope you are not going to use your foreign upbringing as an excuse this time," Mrs. B. said with a disapproving frown. "I'm sure that even in the remotest part of France such behavior would be deemed strange, to put it mildly."

Thinking of the punk hairdos and wild grunge clothing Susannah had seen the last time she'd been in Paris, she doubted anything would seem strange. "I can explain," she repeated. "You see, my husband, Kane, is an . . . inventor. I was merely trying out one of his most recent inventions."

"An inventor? You mean like that Mr. Edison up North I've read about in the newspaper?"

"That's right."

"Your husband is inventing a sound machine?"

"In a manner of speaking, yes."

"There, Gerta." Mrs. B. patted the maid's trembling shoulder reassuringly. "I told you it was nothing to be afraid of, silly girl. Mr. Wilder is an inventor." She drew the word out, as if that might make it easier for the foreign maid to understand. "He is making a sound machine. That's the noise you heard." To Susannah, she said, "You know, I'd be most interested in seeing the machine."

"Oh, my husband doesn't let anyone see his toys until he's finished with them," Susannah hastily stated.

"Toys?" Mrs. B. repeated in confusion.

"That's what I call his inventions," Susannah replied.

"Among other things," Kane interjected mockingly, having just walked in on their conversation. "What's going on here?"

"Nothing, sweetie," Susannah quickly declared. "Gerta walked in while I was listening to your . . . sound machine."

"My sound machine, huh?" Kane said, stalling for time.

"That's right. Naturally, she was frightened seeing me dancing around the room half-dressed like that—"

"Half-dressed?" Kane repeated. Damn. He should have gotten home earlier. Clearly he'd missed a great show here. As it was, he hadn't been able to pick up much information at the tavern, other than the fact that rumor had it that Mrs. Hilton and Whitaker were indeed having an affair. But from what Kane gathered, married men often did that sort of thing in this time period. Apparently, the key was being discreet about the matter.

"I'll tell you about it later," Susannah was saying. "We've cleared everything up now."

Gerta didn't look all that reassured, as Mrs. B. continued trying to explain the meaning of the word *inventions* to the maid.

"I can't leave you alone five minutes without getting into trouble, can I?" Kane declared, once they were upstairs.

"I'll have you know that you were gone much longer than five minutes," she began when Kane interrupted her.

"Missed me, did you?"

"Don't be ridiculous," she retorted.

"So how did you spend your afternoon, aside from terrorizing the poor maid?" he mockingly inquired.

"Actually that kept me pretty busy," she replied in kind.

"I'll bet."

"So what did you find out at the saloon?"

"That the New York baseball teams aren't playing any better in this century than they are in our own."

"It took you four hours to figure that out?" she said.

"Timing me, were you?"

"On the contrary. I had a busy afternoon myself."

"Terrorizing the maid."

"And Mr. Whitaker's law clerk."

"What are you talking about?"

"Oh, nothing, aside from the fact that I met the mysterious Gordon Stevens, the law clerk who keeps a picture of Elsbeth in his wallet. And the man was very nervous. He's definitely hiding something." So was Susannah. She had plans for tonight that she had no intention of telling Kane.

"Maybe he knew about the affair his boss and that Hilton woman are having," Kane said.

"Just because we caught them about to embrace, doesn't mean they're having an affair."

"I agree. Which is why I talked to a few people at the tavern. That's where I heard about their affair."

"And they say *women* gossip!" Susannah said in a huff. "Get a bunch of men together in a bar and watch out. They talk sports and women."

"How do you know that?" Kane demanded.

"I've got two older brothers." Her expression became worried as she thought of her family.

"I miss my family, too," Kane said.

The problem was, his family consisted of a lying younger brother. But Susannah knew that there was no way she could convince Kane of her innocence. In the end, it was her word against his brother's. But when she got back to her own century and her own office, she was going to read the riot act to young Charles Wilder. She'd *make* him tell Kane that he'd been lying about having an affair with her.

Seeing her fierce expression, Kane asked, "What are you thinking?"

How should she answer? That she wanted to drive a stake through his brother's heart—figuratively speaking, of course? She doubted the confession would help her cause any. "I was thinking that if Hayward Whitaker was cheating on his wife, then he had the perfect motive for killing her so he could be with his mistress."

"Him?" Kane repeated. "What about her? She wanted to become the next Mrs. Hayward Whitaker, but she had to get rid of his wife first."

"You don't have a shred of evidence to make that kind of accusation."

"Neither do you," he countered. "Yet it's okay for you to accuse Hayward Whitaker of murder."

CATHIE LINZ                    125

"Women aren't as violent as men."

"And you call me a sexist!"

"Statistics back me up," Susannah said. "You're just accusing her because of what happened with your brother! You see me as the wicked other woman, guilty as sin. And you're doing the same thing to this Hilton woman. Making unfounded accusations. Hurtful accusations that don't hold an ounce of truth to them."

"Are we talking about Mrs. Hilton or about you, here?" he quietly asked.

She looked up and was caught—caught in the seductive web of his gaze, caught wishing for the impossible. Wishing for him to trust her, to believe her. She wanted it so much she couldn't breathe. She tried to read his expression, thinking she saw a matching hope there. A hope for what?

They were interrupted by the simultaneous sounds of the dinner gong and Kane's stomach growling, breaking the sultry tension that had been building between them.

Susannah and Kane both started laughing.

"We'd better go down," Susannah said.

Kane nodded. "I wonder how many dishes Gerta is going to break tonight?"

The answer was three. The maid acted as if she had as many left feet. Susannah could commiserate. She felt rather unsteady herself. Hope had returned to her heart. And she wasn't sure that was a good thing where Kane was concerned.

Despite Gerta's clumsiness in serving it, the meal itself was delicious—cold meat, potato salad, with the promise of fresh fruit for dessert.

Another dish crashed to the floor. With a shake of her head, Mrs. B. had to take over and banish poor Gerta to the kitchen.

Susannah wished she could banish her wayward feelings for Kane as easily.

* * *

Shortly after dinner, Susannah and Kane both retired to their room. Remembering the book their landlady had lent her, Susannah picked it up from the fireplace mantel and sat in the rocking chair by the window to begin reading it.

Kane had muttered something about making flow charts of the suspects and had busied himself writing notes in a notepad he kept in his jacket pocket. "Don't let anyone see you with that ballpoint pen," Susannah warned him, before turning the page.

Instead of responding to her comment, he said, "What are you reading?"

"An etiquette book. This is the neatest thing. I had no idea.... Look... What do you think this means?" She picked up her fan and drew it across her forehead.

"That you're hot. Got a fever, maybe?"

"Wrong. Drawing the fan across my forehead this way means *We are being watched.*"

"By whom?"

"No one. At the moment, anyway. I was just giving you an example. There's an entire silent language used with the fan. Fanning fast means *I am engaged.* Fanning slow means *I am married.*"

"I did notice you've been fanning slow while you've been here."

"And look, there's a hidden language with the parasol, too." She picked it up from its resting place near the door. Checking her book once again, she accidentally dropped the parasol on the floor.

"What does that mean?" he asked.

"That I'm clumsy," she muttered, blushing.

Getting up from his resting place on the bed, he took the book from her, tugging it out of her hands before she could protest. Looking at the page, he said, "Let me see.... Ah, here it is. It says here that dropping your parasol means *I love you.*"

Her heart stopped at the sound of him saying those three words. What would it be like to have him say those words and mean them? Her wistful thoughts were bound to get her into trouble, but she couldn't resist momentarily imagining what it would be like to have Kane love her. Not just to be reluctantly attracted to her, while distrusting and often disliking her. But to have him care for her, confide in her, trust her, love her, kiss her, embrace her, take her to a place she'd never been before.

*He's already taken you someplace you've never been before,* her prosaic side immediately pointed out. *Nineteenth-century Savannah!*

*He* hadn't taken her here, she reminded the inner voice. In fact, he complained that *she'd* brought him. But he had taken her to a misty plane of sensual pleasure—simply by kissing her! Imagining herself making love with him was enough to raise her body temperature another ten degrees and force her to grab her fan again.

"You're fanning yourself quickly," Kane noted. "That means you're engaged."

"It means I'm hot," she stated, fanning herself even faster.

"How are guys supposed to keep track of all these hidden meanings?" Kane wondered aloud as he read the nearly two dozen variations for fan flirtations alone. There were just as many listed for handkerchiefs, gloves, and parasols.

"They didn't have television or radio to distract them."

"And men in our time think *they've* got it hard." *Hard.* Kane winced at his choice of words. Since watching her out of the corner of his eye, he'd gotten more and more aroused just by looking at her. The wrap she was wearing showed her chemise underneath and he could just barely see a hint of the curve of her breast. She had such white skin. Especially when compared to her midnight dark hair, which she'd loosely tied back with a ribbon. Her face was flushed and she was nervously licking her lips in a way that made Kane groan.

He was dying to kiss her. He wanted to throw the book across the room and take her in his arms. Then he wanted to lower her onto the bed they shared and peel every layer of clothing off her, kissing every inch of her creamy skin as he exposed it to his gaze. And he wanted to make her want him as much as he wanted her, watching her brown eyes melt as he slid into her and made her his.

"Um, how is the suspect list coming?" Susannah nervously asked. She had reason to be nervous. There seemed to be a tidal wave of attraction building between her and Kane, all but drowning them and pulling them into its dangerous undertows. Or had she just imagined it? Maybe Kane had merely been thinking about solving the case.

"The suspect list?" Kane repeated. "Right." Returning to the bed, he grabbed his notebook. "Well, we've already got a motive for Elsbeth's death. Now we need to see who had the opportunity. To do that we have to ascertain exactly where in the house both suspects were that night."

"There are *three* suspects," Susannah reminded him. "Don't forget that picture of Elsbeth we found in Gordon Stevens's wallet."

"A picture doesn't make him a suspect. What would he have to gain by Elsbeth's death?" Kane demanded.

"He could have had a dangerous obsession with her. It happens. Quiet, seemingly normal guys create a fantasy life of their own that has nothing to do with reality," she calmly noted.

"Is this your way of saying my brother is living in a fantasy world?"

"I can't think of any other reason for him to lie," she said.

"Okay, have it your way." Her heart leapt. Did that mean he was finally willing to believe her? "We've got three suspects. But I'm sure this Hilton woman did it." He went on to discuss the case, acting as if his brother's name hadn't been mentioned at all, but Susannah was no longer listening.

When would she learn? There was no convincing Kane that his beloved brother was the one at fault, that she was the innocent party.

As Kane got ready for bed, Susannah stayed in the rocking chair, reading her book—or at least pretending to read it.

"Aren't you coming to bed?" he asked.

She shook her head. "You go ahead. I want to read some more."

"Suit yourself," Kane said with a shrug as he got into bed and tugged the draped mosquito netting down on all sides.

The flickering kerosene lamp on the dresser provided the light for Susannah to read by as she waited for Kane to drop off. When she heard the sound Kane made when he was asleep—almost a snore but not quite—she got up and carefully blew out the lamp.

Blue moonlight spilled in through the window, guiding her as she quickly put on the men's black pants and jacket she'd found in the trunk Mrs. B. had gotten from the attic. She paused long enough to dab on some more insect repellent, just to be on the safe side. Then she put a black cap on her head, stuffing her hair inside it before stealing out the door to go check on Hayward Whitaker's whereabouts.

"Follow that cab," Susannah growled. Somehow, she'd never imagined herself saying those words to a sleepy-eyed driver in a horse and carriage. But she'd no sooner gotten to the Whitaker house than she'd seen Hayward furtively leaving the house and taking off in a hired carriage.

"What did you say, sir?" the driver hesitantly inquired.

"You heard me," Susannah snapped, deliberately keeping her voice low and gravelly. After all, she *was* supposed to be impersonating a man. "Follow that cab, er, carriage. Don't lose them, whatever you do. There's an extra five dollars in it for you," she added, at which time the carriage took off like a bat out of hell. You'd have thought she'd just offered him a hundred bucks! Maybe she had—in their currency.

It didn't matter. She had a very strong feeling that something very important was going to happen tonight. And it was going to happen wherever Whitaker was headed. She had to get there in time.

*There* turned out to be the Bonaventure Cemetery, and Susannah's carriage driver warned her about visiting it after dark, claiming the place was haunted.

Knowing she had a ghost—Elsbeth—on her side, Susannah felt no such fear. She hopped out of the carriage and dismissed him. But still, she made her way carefully through the foliage and shadowy headstones toward the carriage Mr. Whitaker had hired. Ghosts might not be a threat, but Whitaker could be. He was no longer in the carriage, but she could see him a short distance away.

There was a full moon tonight, but some clouds were moving in to cut down on the light, which was good. The air was oppressive, thick with the smell of rotting vegetation. The Spanish moss hanging on the massive oak trees lining the lane took on a life of their own in the bluish moonlight, casting ghostly fingers toward the ground.

Susannah was just thinking it was a good thing she didn't scare easily when she was suddenly grabbed from behind. A rough hand placed over her mouth stifled her scream.

# Eight

___

Susannah panicked. She'd been perched behind a head-stone in a cemetery, for God's sake! Who wouldn't have a heart attack when grabbed out of the dark this way? She struggled to get free, her cap falling off her head and her hair tumbling around her, but her attacker held her too tightly for her to escape.

"What the hell do you think you're doing?" a male voice growled in her ear.

It was Kane. And he staggered back as she went limp with relief.

"Don't you dare faint on me," he growled again.

His impatience was like a douse of cold water.

She made a soft noise that sounded like a growl of her own. Kane didn't know whether it was safe to let go of her or not. It certainly wasn't safe to keep holding on to her this way. His arm was around her waist, his hand pressed beneath her left breast. He knew it was her left because he could feel her heart pounding beneath his palm. And he knew it was her breast because he could feel the curve of her soft flesh even through the ridiculous men's clothing she was wearing. In fact, it felt like she wasn't wearing much of anything beneath that clothing.

The feel of her teeth starting to clamp over his hand—the one still covering her mouth—got his attention in a hurry!

"Don't you dare," he warned her menacingly before hastily pulling his hand away. "And don't make any noise, either."

She gave him a look that would have splintered any one of the marble headstones around them. Then she looked for Hayward Whitaker. He'd gone! So had the carriage that had brought him there.

"Where did he go?" she whispered.

"Who?"

"Hayward Whitaker. Why else do you think I'm hiding behind a damned headstone in a cemetery?"

"Beats me."

"I'd like to beat you. Senseless. Why did you have to come here tonight and ruin everything?"

"Wait a second, here. Let me get this straight. You trailed Hayward Whitaker out here to a deserted cemetery? Have you lost your mind?"

"The meeting place was his idea, not mine."

"Who was he meeting?"

"Damned if I know," she countered. "You jumped me before I could see."

Kane made no apology for his actions. Instead he glared at her as they both remained crouched behind the headstone. "I thought that's why we hired the damned detective, for him to do this kind of dirty work."

"I wouldn't have gotten so dirty if you hadn't pounced on me!" she retorted.

"What you were doing was dangerous," Kane said, his voice still a low growl. "What if they'd seen you here? What if they'd been the ones to 'pounce' on you as you so delicately put it? I doubt they'd have let you out of here alive."

She was alive, all right—alive with bolts of electricity shooting through her where his body touched hers. Although Kane had removed his hand from her mouth, his other arm still encircled her. She could feel the warmth of his hand as it rested just beneath her breast, branding her with its searing possessiveness.

"How did you get here?" she demanded, willing her heart to stop beating like a wild thing.

"I saw you leave the boardinghouse. You'd been acting strangely all night," he added parenthetically, "so I followed you in a hired carriage."

"Where is the carriage now?"

"At the gate to the cemetery."

"Great. I'll bet Hayward Whitaker saw it on his way out."

"Normally the cemetery gates are closed during the night. The driver told me that. And he was parked to one side, so no one could see."

"Fine. Let's go question him. Maybe he saw where Hayward was headed."

Reaching for her cap and dusting the dirt off it, she pulled away from him and marched down the lane leading away from the river and back toward the main entrance.

Kane hurried after her. "I can't believe you were stupid enough to sneak out here—"

"I'm not the stupid one. *You* are! I was following a lead—"

"You were putting yourself in danger." He went on a tirade, out of which she heard one sentence above all the others. "How the hell am I supposed to find my way back home if something happens to you?"

"Oh, fine! So now I'm just a ticket back to the twentieth century? How kind of you to be worried about my welfare," she snapped.

"That's not what I meant and you know it."

"I know no such thing," she said as she attempted to pull herself up into the carriage, thoughts of questioning the driver forgotten.

Kane took her by the waist and lifted her, practically tossing her inside. Climbing in after her, he slammed the door shut and banged on the roof to tell the driver to get them moving.

Susannah deliberately ignored him, staring out the window into the moonlit landscape. The hard white road leading back to town threaded ribbonlike in the night.

"We're going to clear this up here and now," Kane began.

She cut him off, the look she tossed him over her shoulder as fiery as the Savannah sunshine. "I already told you that I know exactly what you meant."

"Then know this..." he growled, before pulling her into his arms and kissing her. He was so angry he wasn't thinking straight. Kissing her might have alleviated his anger, but it sure as hell didn't help him think any better. He didn't care. Once he had her in his arms, once he had her soft mouth under his, nothing could stop him—except her resistance.

But she didn't resist.

Susannah meant to meet his anger with fury of her own. Instead, only the passion came through, and was returned in the way his tongue slid between her parted lips to tangle with hers. His need was naked, his hunger openly expressed as he growled her name before tugging her closer.

Susannah slid her fingers through his hair, marveling at the silky texture of it. Her fingernails dug into his shoulders as he nipped her earlobe on his way down her throat. His nimble fingers made short work of unfastening her camisole, undoing ribbons and buttons so that his hands could slip inside to cup her bare breasts in his palm.

Susannah was fiercely glad she hadn't worn a bra that night. She didn't want anything getting in the way of his touch. He was meant to touch her this way and she felt as if she'd waited a lifetime for it to finally happen. Now that it had, the pleasure was even more intense than she could ever have anticipated.

Brushing one thumb over her right nipple, he lowered his head to circle the other one with his tongue, painting erotic pictures with this most seductive of brushes. Shivering with delight, she drew him closer, her fingers sinking into his shoulders as he teased her with his lips before taking her into his mouth.

Her head tilted back against the leather seat as ecstasy swept through her. She didn't know he'd undone the trousers she wore until she felt the heat of his hand against her feminine mound. The thin nylon of her bikini underwear did little to block out his touch, amplifying it instead as he slowly rubbed the heel of his hand up and down, up and down.

The carriage flew over a bump in the road, dislodging her breast from his mouth. Her murmured protest of the loss was integrated into their kiss, as once again their mouths merged with unmitigated passion.

One kiss blended into the next as they experimented with tilts and angles. Susannah didn't realize she was lying on the seat until she felt the smooth leather against her back. Even then, she only noticed her new position with some distant part of her mind. The rest of her attention was focused on the rising heat throbbing deep within her.

Kane was stroking her from collarbone to navel, his fingertips leaving a trail of delight with every passing. And each time, he went a little lower, until his fingers slid beneath the elastic waistband of her bikinis to tantalize her there.

The carriage hit another bump and swayed, shifting his fingers so that they slid down farther, brushing against the secret nub hidden in the crisp curls.

Susannah cried out as the mounting anticipation suddenly snapped, and surges of raw bliss pulsed through her body. Kane kissed her expressions of pleasure from her mouth. His hands were on the fly of his pants when the carriage came to an abrupt halt, tossing him off the seat and onto the floor.

The sudden jolt brought him back to earth in a hurry. Scrambling to his knees, Kane berated himself for his lack of control. What had he been thinking of, trying to seduce her in the nineteenth-century equivalent to the back seat of a car? His anger had taken him over the edge. Her passion had hastened his fall.

At least *she'd* gained some measure of satisfaction, while he was still hard and throbbing, with no relief in sight. His frustration was increased.

Susannah's looking at him with shocked and dazed big brown eyes didn't help matters any, either.

"Do up your jacket," Kane growled as he heard the driver climbing down and coming around to open the carriage door for them.

His curt words burned her soul. Humiliation washed over her, replacing the last lingering tingles of pleasure that might have remained. How could she have let him touch her like that? Why hadn't she fought him off? Instead she'd sunk onto her back and practically offered herself up to him. That was sure to reconfirm his impression of her being a loose woman even further.

How did she explain to him that she hadn't been with a man in more years than she cared to remember? And that there hadn't been many in her lifetime—a grand total of two. Abstinence and celibacy were in, didn't he know that?

Roughly shoving buttons into buttonholes, Susannah managed to get her jacket done up just as the driver opened the door. Flying out of the carriage as if spring-loaded, Susannah dashed up the boardinghouse steps, leaving Kane to deal with paying for the cab.

She hid in the tiny water closet until she regained some self-control. She didn't have a lantern with her. The darkness hid the tears sliding down her cheeks. How was she supposed to face him after what had just happened between them?

Closing her eyes, she prayed for Elsbeth to send her back, to return her to her own time. But there was no magical blue light to zap her home. Instead she sensed a soft regret, as if Elsbeth were—in her own way—trying to give her comfort.

To some degree, it worked. Susannah's tears stopped and her mind started working, attempting to come up with something to say that would disguise her humiliation and return things to normal.

As it was, she didn't have to worry. Kane did what little talking there was when she finally returned to the bedroom they shared.

"What happened in the carriage was a mistake," he stated curtly. "It won't happen again."

Susannah nodded her agreement, before slipping behind the dressing screen and hurriedly ripping the rumpled men's clothing from her body. She took a quick sponge bath, but knew there was little hope of washing away the memory of Kane's touch. Sliding the gown over her head she hurried toward the bed and climbed in, tucking the mosquito netting into the mattress and wishing she could tuck herself into a tiny ball and disappear, as Kane muttered something about going out for a long walk.

Susannah didn't sleep well. She hadn't gotten to sleep until almost three, when Kane had finally returned. He was up and dressed before she opened her eyes the next morning. She came downstairs to find him sitting at the large dining table, along with three new guests at the boarding-house.

"Ah, there you are," Mrs. B. greeted Susannah. "Why, that ensemble looks most becoming on you, dear."

Susannah looked down at the white blouse she wore; the leg-of-mutton sleeves accomplished what shoulder pads did in her era—broadening the shoulders and making the waist look narrower. Of course, a corset was also supposed to physically make the waist narrower, but so far Susannah had managed to avoid wearing one of those.

She wasn't so lucky avoiding Kane's eyes as she walked into the dining room with Mrs. B. One glance and she read the simmering anger and hunger in his blue eyes. And the steely determination.

Susannah's spine stiffened, and her chin lifted as she prepared herself for battle. She was *not* going to turn into a simpering miss. And she wasn't going to put up with his attitude problem. *He* was the one who kissed her in the carriage last night, starting the entire erotic chain reaction. The blame lay at *his* doorstep, not hers.

She preferred being angry with him to the hurt she'd felt last night. Her indignation provided her with a cloak of composure as she greeted the newcomers to whom Mrs. B. was introducing her to.

"These are the Misses Abernathy of Savannah," the landlady was saying. "Miss Agnes and Miss Agatha, may I present Mrs. Susannah Wilder of France."

The two women looked like a history lesson come to life. They had the kind of features Susannah had only seen in paintings—faces etched with life—and they held themselves with a regal air that Susannah could only admire as they courteously nodded their heads at her.

"And this is Professor Dudley Hering of Boston." Mrs. B. repeated her earlier introduction of Susannah.

"Charmed, I'm sure," the professor said, taking her hand and completing a stiff bow over it. He'd risen from his chair the moment she'd first entered the room.

Kane, meanwhile, kept right on eating.

"Your husband was just about to tell us about your life in France," the professor said.

"We wouldn't want to bore you," Susannah replied, not trusting Kane to come up with a halfway believable story. After all, she'd already heard his idea of French—*Regardez la cam-er-a, s'il vous plaît.* She remembered the humor in his rich voice that day as he'd spoken to Mikey.

This morning he wasn't speaking at all; at least, not to her.

If the others around the table noticed the tension between Susannah and Kane, they were too well-bred to make any comment about it.

As far as she was concerned, the new guests couldn't have arrived at a more fortuitous time, as their charming stories helped mitigate the effect of Kane's silent treatment. And anything that could keep her mind off Kane and the intimacies they'd shared in that carriage was a godsend.

"Things are very lively in the last days of November, when the tall, handsome planters from the surrounding plantations come to town," Miss Agatha was saying. "Will you still be here then?"

Susannah shook her head. "We won't be staying that long." She shot Kane a discreet look over the breakfast table, but he continued to give her the silent treatment. Susannah gave him equal measure in return.

*Equal measure...* Susannah had to smile at her own quaint turn of phrase. The truth was that she was starting to think more and more like a native. A part of her felt strangely at home in this time period, with its elegance and grace.

She wasn't at home in these tightly bustled skirts, however. She squirmed slightly in her seat, longing for a pair of jeans, and remembering the men's pants she'd worn to the cemetery last night—when Kane had scared a good ten years off her life before taking her in his arms....

No! She wasn't going to think about it anymore.

Despite those good intentions, after breakfast Susannah realized her willpower was weakening. Kane had taken off without telling her where he was going. It was no good staying inside and brooding about him. She needed to go out.

Mikey accompanied Susannah on her "perambulation," as the Abernathy sisters called it. On a whim, Susannah decided to explore the area along the riverfront, where a virtual forest of masts was formed by the tall sailing ships docked there. The levee was lined with warehouses, which

over a hundred years later would be turned into trendy
boutiques and restaurants as the city's waterfront was re-
habilitated.

In fact, from her hotel window Susannah had been able
to see some of the very same old staircases and wrought-
iron-trimmed brick buildings. Then, as now, the high stair-
ways led to mysterious cubbyholes and alleyways.

"Does this look like France?" Mikey interrupted her
thoughts to ask her as he pointed at the wharf stretched out
below them.

"It certainly is a busy place," she replied.

"It gets much busier in the fall," Mikey claimed. "That's
when they sell most of the cotton and load it. You can hear
the clanking sound of the hoisting crane from morning till
night and the piles of bales reach just about up to heaven, I
reckon."

"That high, huh?" Susannah said, a smile in her voice.

"And the ships waiting to load the cotton are backed up
all the way to... all the way to France!"

Grinning at the boy's exaggeration, she said, "Wow!"

"Are you speaking French again?" Mikey demanded
suspiciously. Without waiting for an answer he said, "We
better be going now. 'Tain't a good thing to be hanging
about the waterfront too long. We might get into trouble."

Susannah knew all about trouble. Trouble, in a nutshell,
was Kane Wilder's middle name.


"Hey, look. There's that fancy redheaded lady you been
asking about," Mikey exclaimed as he and Susannah passed
a dress shop on their way home.

"Hay is for horses, straw is cheaper," Susannah automatically said, even as she noted that Mikey was right. Mrs.
Hilton was inside the shop.

It was a heaven-sent opportunity, and one Susannah
wasn't going to overlook. A small bell over the door tin-
kled as she entered the shop. Mrs. Hilton did not look up,
but remained engrossed in a conversation with the dress-

maker. In the end, Susannah had to literally bump into the other woman to get her attention.

"Why, hello there. Fancy bumping into you here," Susannah said with a brilliant smile. "We met at Hayward Whitaker's office the other day," she added when the other woman appeared to be pretending not to know her. "My name is Susannah."

Like so many before her, Mrs. Hilton's gaze fastened on the garnet necklace and matching earrings Susannah was wearing. This time Susannah made no comment about the other woman's interest. To her surprise, Mrs. Hilton began speaking to her in fluent French. "I have heard people say that you are from France. Is this true?"

"Yes, it's true," Susannah answered in French. "Did Hayward talk to you about me?"

The other woman's eyes flashed with jealousy. "I thought you did not know Hayward."

"I don't. You appeared to know him pretty well, though," Susannah added.

Mrs. Hilton ignored her observation. "Where in France do you make your home?"

"A very small place."

"Your parents were American?"

"They still *are* American," Susannah replied. "They are very much alive and healthy."

"Really? They must be very old by now."

Susannah glared at the other woman, not appreciating that comment one bit.

Then Mrs. Hilton switched back to English just as abruptly. "You are a friend of Andrea Hall in New York?"

"Her name is *Althea* Hall," Susannah said.

"You are a friend of hers?"

"Why the curiosity, madam?"

"Forgive me," Mrs. Hilton apologized with all the sincerity of a carpetbagger. "I was under the impression that you were curious about me and I thought that turnabout was fair play."

"But naturally I would be curious about a woman with your fashion sense and beauty," Susannah returned, deciding to appeal to the other woman's vanity. "As you can see, I am but a poor peasant when it comes to such matters. My parents were of an artistic nature—" *Well, her dad was a painter. A housepainter.* "And they did not teach me in such social matters."

"Your father is an artist? I visited Paris a few years ago and saw some of the paintings of that awful school they are calling Impressionism. They are fools. Such garish colors."

"If I were you, I'd buy as many Monets as I could afford," Susannah advised, knowing full well the other woman would ignore her.

Which she did. "I can understand your saying that since, as you say, you know little about matters such as correctness of taste or refinement. Where did you come upon such a gown as you are wearing now? Surely not from France?"

"No, not from France. From my landlady's attic," Susannah cheerfully replied. "You see, our trunks of clothing were stolen when we reached the train station and we had to rely on the kindness of strangers in matters regarding our clothing. Until we can get our own made, that is. Come to think of it, I think I saw a store near here that advertises ready-made gowns."

Mrs. Hilton sniffed disapprovingly. "I would never wear such a thing."

"Would you rather I kept wearing what I have on?"

Mrs. Hilton shook her head. "I'd best go with you and guide you," she stated firmly. "You have to watch these shopkeepers."

Susannah beamed. "You're so kind." This was a great opportunity to talk more to Mrs. Hilton. While the other woman was an opinionated snob, that didn't make her a murderer. Besides, women tended to let down their defenses while shopping. Susannah just had to make sure *she* wasn't the one getting caught in any lies.

Mikey got that long-suffering look on his face that he wore whenever they went into a store. He promised to wait outside and looked relieved not to have been forced inside.

Since Susannah had no intention of getting caught wearing her twentieth-century bra and bikini beneath her camisole and petticoats, she made some excuse not to try on every gown Mrs. Hilton suggested. As Susannah looked over the calicoes, satins, silks and serges, she plied the other woman with questions about her life: Did Mrs. Hilton have many friends? Did she miss her husband? Did she see herself ever getting married again?

The one question Susannah wanted to ask and couldn't was: *Did you push Elsbeth down those steps?*

"Are you one of those nickel-nursers?" Mrs. Hilton finally demanded in exasperation when Susannah turned down yet another dress, saying it was too expensive.

"Excuse me?"

"One of those persons for whom it is difficult if not impossible to part from their money, only buying items if they are on sale."

It was true that in New York, Susannah did get most of her clothes from outlet stores. So she nodded.

Mrs. Hilton sniffed her disapproval. "Every two years I go to Paris and have my wardrobe designed by Charles Worth himself."

Susannah was impressed. Judging by the prices at this store—$250 for a sage green silk street dress—Susannah imagined the gowns in New York or Paris cost even more, especially at the House of Worth, the supreme dictator of fashion. This at a time when the average worker earned no more than five hundred dollars a year and rent on a suite of rooms was ten dollars a month.

Susannah got to wondering exactly how wealthy Mrs. Hilton's first husband had been—and how quickly the woman had gone through his money.

By the end of their time together, Susannah came away with the information that Mrs. Lucille Hilton had many acquaintances, no friends, didn't miss her rich husband one iota, was *not* a nickel-nurser, and definitely saw herself as getting married again. Susannah also came away from the encounter with a pair of walking shoes that looked like boots and felt like butter. She had to have them; her velvet flats had never recovered from her jaunt into the cemetery and she'd been getting some unwelcome attention from ruffians because of her ankles showing.

Susannah also came away with her feelings about Mrs. Hilton's connection to Elsbeth's death unchanged. She just didn't think this woman had done it.

Granted that at times, Mrs. Hilton had looked guilty and acted uneasy, just as that law clerk, Gordon Stevens, had. But perhaps that was because both of them knew of Hayward's dastardly deed. Perhaps they feared for their own safety. After all, if a man killed his own wife, there was no telling what other crimes he might commit.

After dinner that evening, Kane announced he was going out for a walk. Susannah retired to her room alone. It was hot and the humidity was stifling. So was the tension between herself and Kane. How much longer could this last? She was reaching the end of her rope.

Unable to stand the heavy layers of clothing a moment longer, Susannah peeled down to her petticoat and camisole. After putting on another layer of insect repellent, she blew out the lamp—she still avoided the gas wall fixture like the plague—and opened the shutters to what little breeze there was.

Aiming the rocking chair toward the window, she sat down, remembering the sounds of summer in her own era—car horns, police and fire sirens, airplanes and car alarms, her neighbors in apartment 15 who always had the stereo blaring and who argued at the top of their lungs. She'd never realized how much noise there actually was until she heard this . . . peaceful silence.

Yet it wasn't a vacuum without sound. She could hear the rustle of the palmetto leaves in the slight breeze, the chirping of crickets and tree frogs. And, in the distance, the rumble of thunder.

A storm was brewing. Susannah could feel it, sense it in the air. The breeze stopped and the air went still with that brooding anticipation that precedes turbulent weather.

She had her petticoat hiked up to her thighs, her feet resting on the wide seat to get the most airflow possible.

A flash of heat lightning illuminated the room just as Kane entered it. He saw her frozen in that brief moment, sitting like a goddess on her throne, her hair piled on top of her head, with tendrils sliding down her nape, her lovely legs ivory in the flash of light. The storm was rolling in, getting closer.

Another sheet of heat lightning lit the room as he moved closer. Sensing his presence, she turned to look at him. He saw the questions in her eyes. And he knew the only answer.

"Isn't it time we both stopped fighting and just gave in?" Kane murmured before lifting her out of the rocking chair and kissing her.

# Nine

Lightning flashed, not only in the night sky but in Susannah's very soul. There was no anger in Kane's kiss. Instead there was acceptance and a hunger too overwhelming to ignore a second longer. She knew the feeling well, for she felt the same way herself.

Their attempts to fight the growing attraction were as futile as trying to stop the rain. It poured from the sky the way his kisses poured over her face as he caressed her eyes, her temples, pausing to swirl his tongue in her ear before returning to the wet promise of her parted lips.

With the acceptance of their mutual surrender came a newfound sense of anticipation. For now, no part of their psyches was bothered with fighting. Instead, all efforts were devoted to increasing satisfaction.

Susannah poured her heart and soul into their kiss, telling him with her lips and caressing hands what she couldn't say in words. That she loved him. That he was the only man for her. That no one had ever made her feel the way he had.

She wanted to believe that the way he was kissing her said the same. The tenderness in his touch was balm to her bruised heart. He whispered her name with delightful approval, not censure.

Kane slid his hand up her thigh, lifting her lacy petticoat out of his way as he did so. He took his time, pausing to trail his fingertips over her sensitive skin as if he took delight in the mere act of touching her.

Susannah was doing some exploring of her own, fumbling with the buttons on his linen shirt, tugging his shirttails out of his pants before remembering he was wearing suspenders. She slid her fingers beneath the waistband of his pants to grapple with the suspenders' button fastenings. When they proved stubborn she tried the fastenings at the back of the waistband, but was distracted by the muscular firmness of his tush. Afraid he'd think her too bold if she caressed him there, she hurriedly undid the suspenders, which almost hit her and him in the head as they flew forward.

To her delight, Kane actually laughed, his devilish gambler's smile something she'd missed intensely the past few days. The gleam in his blue eyes was positively wicked as he peeled off his clothing.

She blinked at what he wore underneath. They looked like biking shorts, cut off at midthigh. And wonderful thighs they were, too—lean and muscular.

Seeing her gaze, Kane explained, "I bought a few pairs of men's drawers and then borrowed a pair of Mrs. B.'s scissors to cut them shorter. I got too hot."

"I know the feeling," Susannah murmured, fanning herself with her hand.

Thunder rolled around the room, echoing off the walls. It only mirrored the thunder of her own heart. Lightning flashed again, illuminating Kane in all his splendor as he discarded the underwear and stood before her wearing nothing but a grin.

Holding out his arms to her, he whispered her name.

She came to him without regrets. She returned his kiss with equal passion, matching the thrust of his tongue with an ingenious twist of her own. She helped him undo the ribbons and buttons on her camisole, before tossing it aside. The room was dark as she guided his big hands to the fullness of her breasts. She gasped her approval as he cupped her, rubbing his thumbs over the rosy peaks.

He made love to her with his mouth, the rhythmic thrusting of his tongue mimicking the joining that was yet to come. Then his lips lowered to her bare breasts to seduce her there, as his hands shifted southward to untie the drawstrings holding up her petticoat. Once they were undone, the lacy cotton slid to the floor, leaving her wearing nothing but her bikini underwear. Her fingers slid into his hair as he knelt before her and erotically ravished her through the thin nylon—with lips and tongue that knew exactly how and where to create havoc.

Her fingers tightened as bolts of raw pleasure swept through her, as sharp as the lightning bolt zigzagging across the sky outside their window.

Unable to stand another moment, Susannah sank to her knees. Face-to-face with Kane, she slanted her lips over his as she reached down to take him in her hand, caressing him with stroking fingers. He was hard, hot steel overlaid with velvet. When her thumb brushed the very tip of his masculinity, he stiffened and, groaning her name, moved away from her.

"Wait!" he gasped.

"What's wrong?"

"Nothing." Cupping her face with his hands, he kissed her reassuringly but very briefly. "I've got a condom in my wallet."

He grimaced at the bluntness of his declaration.

Susannah just smiled. "Then go get it. It's certainly not doing your wallet any good."

He did. And while he was doing that, Susannah moved from the floor where they'd been kneeling to the bed where she removed her bikini underwear while waiting for him to join her. He did so a moment later, his fingers trembling as he removed the latex condom from its wrapper.

"There's no hurry," she murmured seductively. "After all, we've only waited a hundred and eleven years for this."

"It feels like it," he growled in agreement.

"It feels wonderful," she whispered as she reached out to help him slip on and slowly unroll the condom.

"Enjoying playing with my...toys, are you?" he asked in a sexy whisper.

"I'd enjoy it more if you were...mmm," she purred as he slid his finger inside her inner passage for a few teasing strokes. "If you put your toys where they belong."

"And where would that be?"

"Here." She guided him home, slipping her hands around his hips to the small of his back as he came to her in a slow, sliding drive, not pausing until he was lodged deep within her.

"How does that feel?" he whispered in her ear, shifting against her with the slightest of twists.

She nipped his shoulder to pay him back for his darkly erotic teasing.

"Or do you like it this way better?" He rocked his hips against hers.

She saw the flare of passion darken his blue eyes as she tightened around him. No more words were spoken as she lifted her hips and he began rocking against her in a pagan rhythm as old as time itself—the sensual glide in, the blissful friction of the slide back.

The pace picked up as Susannah gasped his name and held on to him. A firestorm of anticipation was building inside her, the undulations spiraling tighter, lifting her to a dizzying peak of excitation, before suddenly snapping free and sending her into a clenching free-fall of sensual rapture. The quivering, swelling waves rippled and then thundered through her, propelled her from this world to another.

Only when Kane felt her climax did he focus on his own satisfaction, shouting her name as he stiffened, joining her in that blissful free-fall.

"That was worth waiting a hundred and eleven years for," Susannah dreamily murmured sometime later.

When Kane made no reply, she propped herself up on an elbow to study his face. "What are you thinking?"

"That I've never met anyone like you."

"Is that good or bad?"

He tenderly brushed his hand down her bare arm until his fingers were entwined with hers. Lifting their joined hands, he kissed her knuckles with courtly gentleness. "It's good," he whispered. "Very, very good."

She smiled her relief. "I can only think of one way it could get better."

"How's that?" His words were muffled as he was engrossed with sliding his tongue into the sensitive valley between her thumb and index finger.

"By having an air conditioner. Despite that storm, it's still sultry."

Sultry as in incredibly humid. Horror-hair weather. Susannah knew her hair was acting up—other women's hair flowed like a cloud over a pillow. She was certain hers looked more like a thunderhead.

As if reading her thoughts, Kane stopped seducing her fingers long enough to reach out and twine his hand around a swath of her dark wavy hair. "You have the most incredible hair," he murmured in amazement.

"Yeah, I know. It's awful."

"No, it's not. It's beautiful."

He kissed the look of amazement from her face before jumping out of bed.

"Where are you going?" she asked.

"It's a surprise."

"It'll be a surprise for the rest of the household if they catch you running around with no clothes on. It's only nine o'clock at night, I'm sure they aren't all in bed yet."

"Don't worry." He tugged on his pants, and hurriedly buttoned his shirt but did not put on his suspenders. "I'll be right back," he promised her. "Don't move until I return."

It was too hot to move.

True to his word, he came back shortly, carrying a bowl.

"Tell me you brought me coffee ice cream and I'll love you forever." The truth was that she loved him, no matter what.

"I brought you something even better."

Susannah couldn't imagine anything better than coffee ice cream, unless it was a lemon ice-cream soda, and that wouldn't fit in a bowl. But chunks of ice did.

"Ice?" she murmured.

Kane nodded, taking one of the irregularly shaped pieces and gently running it over her flushed face. "I got it from the icebox in Mrs. B.'s kitchen."

Susannah closed her eyes at the blissful coolness he was creating. But the coolness was only skin-deep, for inside she felt a fire returning to life.

Kane was mesmerized by the teardrop-shaped drop of water meandering down her neck, heading for the smooth indention above her collarbone. He could wait no longer. He leaned down to capture the runaway waterdrop with his tongue.

"Oh!" Susannah exclaimed, amazed at the streak of excitement Kane had created by the mere touch of his tongue.

Kane skimmed the ice cube over every inch of her bare body. He didn't miss one inlet or curve. From the hollow behind her ear, to the instep of her foot. From the tip of her finger to the pulse at her wrist and inner elbow, to the underside of her breast, to the circular indentation of her navel. . . .

He spent a good three minutes around her navel before meandering downward. She gasped as he cooled her with the ice and warmed her with his tongue. She clenched the sheet in her hands, her head thrashing at the darkly exciting sensations sweeping through her.

Lifting his head, he whispered, "I'm making you all hot and bothered again. I'll have to cool you down once more," he said, his look one of grave determination embroidered with hungry passion. And so he started all over, with another piece of ice, from her temples to her toes.

A blinding flash of lightning filled the room, distracting Kane.

"There's another storm coming," he noted.

"You bet there is," Susannah murmured, finally having enough breath to speak. "And it's starting right here."

Taking the melting ice from his hands, she slipped it over his chest, sliding it around his nipples, which immediately hardened.

Intrigued, she wondered if other parts of his anatomy would respond similarly.

"Don't even think about it," he warned her, scooping her up in his arms and taking her over to the wide rocking chair that was placed near the open window. He only paused long enough to grab another condom on the way.

Sitting on the rocking chair, he settled her over his bare lap so that she was facing him. She felt his arousal moving against her.

"You've left your toys out again," she sexily chastised him even as she made herself more comfortable, her bare legs bracketing him, her bent knees resting against the back of the chair.

She kissed his jaw even as he was grappling with the condom, ripping it from its container with his teeth and hurriedly putting it on. There wasn't room for him to see what he was doing but he voiced no complaint. Instead he told her in a rough and husky whisper exactly what he was going to do to her any second now....

A flash of lightning lit their way as, at his urging, she guided him to her, gasping as he came into her, filling the aching void. But there was much more joy to come. This time the pleasure was even more intense than last time, the friction even greater. It was incredible!

Thunder growled outside. Growling her name, Kane kept his feet on the ground, and slowly set the chair rocking.

Her eyes met his in startled delight—as the chair rocked back, she slid forward, until he was embedded even deeper within her. And when the chair rocked forward, she slipped back. The motion created by him moving inside her was simply awesome and beyond anything she'd ever experienced before. Kane's clasped hands rested on the small of her back and he tightened his hold on her as he made good on his whispered promises.

A sudden gust of wind blew the rain in through the open window. Susannah felt the cool raindrops hitting her skin, sliding down her spine, contrasting sharply with the pulsing warmth lodged within her. The combination took her to another plateau of pleasure.

Throwing her head back, she clung to the wooden back of the chair, her fingers curling tighter as the inner ecstasy continued to grow. The ensuing arch of her back placed her full breasts within easy reach of Kane's seductive mouth. The renegade swirl of his tongue as he laved her nipples aroused the tender tips to taut attention. Lifting his head, he then blew on her dampened skin before lowering his head and starting the process all over again.

This time the tugging motion of his mouth coincided with the sliding thrust as he tilted the rocking chair way back, thrusting upward with his hips and impaling her. Working on instinct, Susannah slid her feet around to the small of his back and braced them there, keeping Kane right where he was as the ecstasy crescendoed. The moment was frozen in time, witnessed by the heavens above and captured by the lightning cleaving the sky. A rumble of thunder drowned out most of her breathless scream as she found heavenly satisfaction.

Feeling her tightening around him, Kane surrendered to his own shuddering climax.

"You want to what?" Kane asked in husky amazement.

"We need to burn that condom you took off."

"The blasted thing was on inside out. What good is a ribbed condom if you put it on inside out?"

"It felt just fine to me," she said with a catlike grin of satisfaction. "Better than fine. Incredible, in fact!"

"Is that why you want to burn it?"

"You can't use it again and there is no other sure way to dispose of it here. I doubt that latex has even been invented yet. So you'd better burn both those condoms you used tonight. After all, you can't leave twentieth-century evidence like that lying about."

"I didn't plan on leaving them just lying about," he grumbled.

"Better safe than sorry. I've been moving that fire screen and burning all the rest of the twentieth-century trash in a sheet of newspaper in the fireplace."

Seeing the wisdom of such a move, Kane did as she suggested.

Watching him, Susannah was sorry to see the sucker go up in smoke. "How many condoms do you have left?"

Kane checked his wallet on the way back from the fireplace.

"A few."

"Then we'd better save them for later."

"Good idea."

Wrapping a sheet around her, he tucked her onto his lap, her head resting on his bare shoulder as they watched the rest of the storm pass by. Susannah fell asleep with the knowledge lodged deep in her heart that she loved this man, and would love him forever.

* * *

"I have a feeling things are going to start moving very quickly on this case," Oliver told Kane and Susannah when they checked in with him for a progress report a few days later.

"Great. Now I've got two of you making decisions based on *feelings*."

"There are worse things," Susannah said.

Kane nodded and gave her one of his trademark grins. "I suppose there are."

Worse things... Susannah wondered if Kane believed her now about her not having been involved with his brother. She was afraid to ask him outright, not wanting to ruin this magical time together. He'd acted as if he were in love with her, showing her new ways of making love, delighting her with his tender creativity, spending his time with her and sharing confidences.

The days raced by. She didn't want this time to end. But she was running out of her heart pills; there were now only three left. And they'd used all but one of Kane's condoms. They were also running short of money, Kane had told her. *Real* short.

"This case has turned out to be one of my most challenging," Oliver was saying.

Kane knew all about *challenging*. Challenging was falling for the woman his brother loved.

Susannah had been skirting the piano for her entire stay at the boardinghouse, but the next afternoon she could resist no longer. Mrs. B. had told her that guests were invited to play. And Kane wasn't there to see her make a fool of herself. He'd gotten a note two hours ago and said he had to go out. She'd teasingly asked him if the letter had been from Polly. Kane had kissed her with enough passion to convince her that he had no energy left over for anyone else. And then he'd told her so, before putting on his bowler and heading out the door.

Leaving Susannah behind . . .

Sighing, she trailed her fingers over the keyboard. It had been so long since she'd played. She sat down and, settling her new Victorian shoes on the foot pedals, started picking out a few tunes, including "The Piano Man" by Billy Joel, before remembering that the Grammy-award winner had gotten her in enough trouble as it was. Gerta still kept her distance and crossed herself three times whenever she saw Susannah.

"That's an unusual tune," Professor Hering observed from the doorway. "Almost has an African tonal quality to it. Is it an old slave spiritual from the cotton fields, perhaps?"

*Nope, it's just rock and roll,* Susannah thought to herself with a grin.

"I play a bit myself," the professor went on to say. "Perhaps you would allow me . . . ?"

Nodding, she changed places with him. He opened the sheet music and chose a piece. "This is one of my favorites by Stephen Foster. Perhaps you've heard it?"

He started playing "My Old Kentucky Home."

By the time he was through, the Abernathy sisters had joined them in the front parlor and were standing around the piano singing the next Foster selection, "Jeanie with the Light Brown Hair." As Mrs. B. added her clear soprano to the chorus of voices, Susannah got a lump in her throat. In this time period, music was a group effort, without the solitary headphones that cut you off from the rest of society. When the professor launched into a robust version of "Oh! Susanna," in her honor, even Mikey was present to join in.

Kane walked in as they finished up the final chorus. Susannah could tell from his face that something momentous had occurred.

Hurrying over to him, she said, "What happened?"

"We need to talk upstairs."

Nodding, she made her excuses to the group.

Gathering her light blue calico skirt in one hand, she rushed upstairs, glad that today she was wearing one of the older, fuller skirts. Since she'd stayed inside, she'd gotten away with wearing a white blouse with the sleeves rolled up and no jacket. As always, she wore her great-grandmother's garnet jewelry set. Her hand sought the necklace as if for reassurance. "What is it? What's happened?" she repeated the second she stepped foot into their room.

Closing the door, Kane said, "It's news about Elsbeth's murderer. We've cracked the case."

"You have?"

He nodded. "That note I got earlier was from Oliver. He and the police and I went over to Mrs. Hilton's place."

"Mrs. Hilton!"

"That's right. A servant came forward after Oliver started investigating her husband's death, saying she remembered the strange smell of almonds in the medicine that Mrs. Hilton had her give her husband. The doctor emphatically stated that the medicine he prescribed would have no such smell—but arsenic would. Upon confrontation, Mrs. Hilton broke down and confessed."

"To killing Elsbeth?" Susannah asked.

"Well, no. Not yet. But it's only a matter of time. And speaking of time, we need to get back to our own century. Better get your rented clothes on and gather up your stuff for the trip back," he said as he hurriedly changed into the clothes he'd time traveled in. "Or should I say the trip forward?"

Did he have to look so happy about it? Couldn't he have shown some regret at leaving this magical place where they'd fallen in love? Or was it only the magical place where *she* had fallen in love, while he'd merely had sex with her?

Not that there had been anything the least bit *merely* about what they'd shared. But he still hadn't declared his feelings for her. Susannah's smile was bittersweet at the old-fashioned nature of her words. This was an era when men declared their love and wooed their women. It was also a time when women had few rights and were still considered men's property in many states.

She'd done what Elsbeth had wanted her to do—to clear Elsbeth's name of the accusation of having committed suicide. If Susannah had fallen in love with Kane along the way, she had no one to blame but herself.

Regarding Elsbeth, Susannah was still having a hard time accepting the idea that Mrs. Hilton was guilty of killing her. She silently appealed to the ghost for confirmation but got the distinct impression that Elsbeth honestly didn't know who had pushed her, she only knew she hadn't fallen down those stairs by herself.

"I need to go check with Oliver at his office," Kane was saying. "See if Mrs. Hilton has confessed to Elsbeth's death yet. I'll be back in an about an hour."

"I'll go with you."

"No. You stay here. I'd feel better knowing you were okay. Besides, you need to settle our bill with Mrs. B. and tell her we'll be leaving tonight. We're going home."

Drifting up from downstairs were the sounds of voices continuing their appreciation of Foster's greatest hits by singing "Old Folks at Home."

Kane absently pecked Susannah on the cheek as he rushed back out again. She sank onto the rocking chair, her thoughts in a turmoil. They were going back home. She should be glad. And she was. But she was also sad. And apprehensive.

It wasn't as if they were jumping a 727 from LaGuardia. What if Elsbeth didn't have the power to get them back to their own time? What if they were stuck in the Victorian era? What if they landed in the wrong time? When you traveled you missed connections all the time. Or lost your luggage. But landing twenty years or so off base could be devastating in their situation.

It didn't take her long to gather up their belongings. She carefully checked the room, making sure that nothing incriminating was left behind. Then she changed out of her skirt and blouse into the rented red velvet dress she'd worn what felt like so long ago.

Chronologically, it had only been less than two weeks ago. Spiritually, it felt like a lifetime.

After doing up her side zipper, she came back into the room, automatically reaching for the parasol and her borrowed hat before remembering that where she was going, she wouldn't need them. Taking them downstairs, she returned them to Mrs. B. and broke the news of their imminent departure.

"I'm sorry not to have given you more warning," Susannah told her as they sat on a Victorian bench in the far corner of what was in effect a greenhouse-conservatory out the back of the parlor. "I never did get around to touring that scientific kitchen of yours, but I'm sure it's lovely. And please thank Cook for giving me that recipe for boiled turkey with oyster sauce. It truly was delicious the way she prepared it."

"But where are you off to in such a great hurry? And so late—it's almost time for the evening meal. It will be dark before you know it. The weather outside has been most peculiar all day. There is such a chill in the air, and the mist coming off the river is making travel difficult."

"We're going home," Susannah said.

"Back to France? But there's no boat leaving Savannah at this late hour."

"Kane has made special arrangements. We've had word...and we must leave right away."

"I shall miss you," Mrs. B. said.

Susannah hugged the woman, before handing her the hat and parasol she'd borrowed. "And I want you to have these boots, also. I know we're of a similar size."

"But you just bought these boots," Mrs. B. protested.

"I know. But I can't use them at home." Actually, she could—this style was all the rage now—but she was afraid that wearing anything from this time might prevent them from making the leap to their own century. "I want you to

have them. As a sign of my gratitude for all you've done
during our visit here.''

Mrs. B. reached out and a second later the two women
were in a tearful embrace.

"What's all this?" Professor Hering inquired.

"Mrs. Wilder is leaving us," Mrs. B. said, wiping the
corners of her eyes with her apron.

Whereupon Susannah said her goodbyes to the Abernathy sisters, Professor Hering, and of course, Mikey.

"I'll never forget you," Mikey said, indulging in a momentary show of affection by giving her a quick, fierce hug
while whispering in her ear, "And I'll never tell nobody
about that magic card of your husband's I seen. And I won't
steal wallets no more. And I'll miss you," he added in a
choked voice before running out of the room.

"I'll miss you, too, Mikey," Susannah murmured.

She'd miss them all. The Abernathy sisters reciting the
history of Savannah or relishing the latest sentimental novel
by Mrs. Southworth, the professor proudly bragging about
his young country's many accomplishments or playing
Stephen Foster melodies on the piano, Mrs. B. raising her
eyebrows and trying to give motherly fashion advice in the
kindest way possible, and Mikey. Susannah blinked away
tears. She'd miss Mrs. B. and Mikey most of all.

"What do you mean, there's a complication?" Kane demanded, upon reaching Oliver's office.

"There's no need to shout, my good fellow. I haven't lost
my hearing yet."

"Just your memory. Mrs. Hilton confessed to killing
Elsbeth," Kane reminded the detective.

"Actually, she only confessed to killing her husband, if
you'll recall."

"What happened after I left?"

"Well, you remember the scenario as we knew it. We had
an alibi for Hayward Whitaker."

Kane nodded impatiently. "He was in the living room at
the time of Elsbeth's death, with a maid who had been

called in to start a fire in that room. The maid swears she was with Hayward when they heard the sound of Elsbeth screaming and falling down the stairs. Mrs. Hilton was supposedly still in the study but no witnesses could place her there at the exact moment.''

''That's right.''

''And now what's happened? Has the maid recanted her story? Was Whitaker the one who did it?''

''No, the maid is not changing her story. But she did add an interesting piece of information.''

''Which was?''

''When we went over her story again, this time she happened to mention in passing that Mr. Whitaker's law clerk had briefly stopped by earlier in the evening with some papers to give to Mr. Whitaker.''

''Gordon Stevens?''

''That's right.''

Kane's skin chilled as he remembered Susannah telling him not to forget there were *three* suspects. *He could have had a dangerous obsession with her. It happens. Quiet, seemingly normal guys create a fantasy life of their own that has nothing to do with reality.*

''And what does Gordon Stevens have to say about this?'' Kane asked.

''That's just the problem. He seems to have disappeared.''

''Disappeared?''

''That's correct. And what's more, Mr. Whitaker says the papers Gordon Stevens brought that evening were not of sufficient importance for the clerk to have made a special trip on a Sunday evening.''

Kane swore softly. ''Does Gordo know we're on to him?''

''Excuse me?''

''Gordon Stevens. Does he know about our suspicions? Does he know we're looking for him?''

''I can't say for certain at this point, but deduction would lead one to believe that he does, judging by his recent disappearance.''

"I've got to get back to the boardinghouse."

"I'll come with you," Oliver interjected. "Perhaps your wife will have some insight into the situation. She does seem to have a sixth sense about these things. She never did believe that Mrs. Hilton was guilty."

"I know. Come on, let's hurry. I don't feel comfortable with Susannah there and this nut on the loose."

"Nut?"

"Maniac, weirdo. Come on, let's go."

Kane set almost a jogging pace back to the boardinghouse, only to find that Susannah was gone.

"Gone? What do you mean, gone?" Kane demanded of a startled Mrs. B. "Where did she go?"

"She didn't tell me. I wanted her to take Mikey with her. The professor offered to accompany her, but she refused both offers. She left shortly after supper. As soon as she got that note, in fact."

Kane pounced on that bit of information. "What note?"

"The one that came for her."

"Who sent it?"

"I'm sure I don't know."

"I do," Mikey piped up from his seat on the top step of the stairway.

"What are you doing out of bed at this time of night?" Mrs. B. chastised him.

"What makes you think you know where Mrs. Wilder went, Mikey?" Oliver asked the young boy.

"'Cause I saw the note, that's why."

"I didn't know you could read," Mrs. B. said in amazement.

"I've been teaching him," Oliver said.

"And your name is?" Mrs. B. inquired.

"Oliver Ogilvie at your service, ma'am."

"Can we get the pleasantries over with later," Kane said impatiently. "Where did she go?" he demanded of Mikey.

"To the bridge."

"What bridge?"

"I couldn't read the name in the note."

"How many bridges are there in Savannah?" Kane turned to ask Oliver. "More than one?"

"I'm afraid so."

"Great."

"I reckon it would help if I showed you the note, then?" Mikey said.

Kane grabbed it out of the boy's hand before gripping his shoulder in a sign of appreciation. "Thanks, kid. You done good."

"Thanks." Mikey beamed. "Then I can come rescue her with you?"

There was a moment of silence as Kane hurriedly read the note, which had supposedly been sent on his behalf and listed the time and place to meet him. "No, you can't come with us," Kane finally replied. Seeing the youngster's crestfallen expression, he added, "Oliver and I need you to stay here and protect Mrs. B. and to wait to see if Susannah should come back here."

"Oh, my!" Mrs. B. exclaimed. "You don't think we're in any danger, do you? Could it be those ruffians who stole your luggage when you first came to town, do you think?"

Kane's expression darkened. "I have a suspicion of who wrote this note, and I don't aim on letting him get away with it."

"We'll hail a cab immediately," Oliver said, putting on his hat and bowing to Mrs. B. "I hope we can meet again under more auspicious circumstances. Good evening, ma'am."

Kane was already outside—on the corner, sticking two fingers into his mouth for a piercing whistle that always worked whenever he was in Manhattan. Hopefully it would work to get a carriage here, too.

When Kane felt a hand on his shoulder, he thought it was Oliver joining him. Instead it was one of the men he'd played poker with that first night—J. P. Bellows. "I'll take that watch from you now," J.P. said.

"What are you talking about?"

"Ah, putting up a fight, are you? I thought you might. So I brought along a little muscle to convince you."

The man looked seven feet tall and about as wide.

"What's going on here?" Oliver demanded as he finally joined Kane.

"Let's get him," J.P. ordered.

Kane couldn't believe this was happening. His anger at Gordon Stevens spilled over to include J.P. and his henchman. They were in his way. Waiting until the last minute to step out of the hulk's way, Kane reached for the man's neck. A second later, his foe lay in a crumpled heap on the sidewalk.

Meanwhile, Oliver was in the midst of an old-fashioned fisticuffs with J.P. A firm upper right to the chin and the other man joined his hired hand on the ground just as a carriage finally pulled up.

"You go on ahead," Oliver told Kane. "I'll wait for the authorities to come and deal with these miscreants. I'll catch up with you at the bridge. Go, before it's too late!"

Susannah approached the deserted bridge with some trepidation. She wasn't real fond of heights. The last time she'd been on a bridge had been when a couple of friends of hers wanted her to videotape them bungee-jumping off one. She'd aimed the camera down and looked the other way.

She heard a noise ahead of her. Squinting into the heavy mist she said, "Kane, is that you?"

A man materialized a mere foot in front of her. The man wasn't Kane. It was Gordon Stevens. "Your husband won't be meeting you here after all, Mrs. Wilder," the law clerk said. "You won't be seeing him . . . or anyone else."

# Ten

—

"**I** won't be seeing anyone?" Susannah repeated in confusion. "You mean because this fog is so thick?"

"No, I mean you won't be seeing anyone because you've been inquiring into matters that are none of your concern."

Her heart sank and the hair at the back of her neck went funny, the way it did whenever she faced danger. "What matters might you be referring to?"

"Don't play me for a fool. That's what *she* did."

"Who?"

"Elsbeth. But you know that already. You knew that I had to push her down those stairs."

"You!"

"She laughed at me, you see. I loved her and she laughed at me. So you can understand why I had to do what I did."

Susannah hurriedly assured him, "Oh, I understand." What she understood was that she had to get out of there, but fast! Gordon Stevens was a man who'd clearly gone over the edge.

She shifted away from him, but he shot his hand out and fastened it around her arm in a painful grip.

"You weren't thinking of going somewhere, were you, Mrs. Wilder?" he asked in the cordial voice of a man inquiring after a neighbor's health. "Because I couldn't allow that. You know too much."

"No, I don't. I didn't know it was you...."

"No? That's a pity. Because you know *now* and that makes you a dangerous liability." Tugging on her arm, he began drawing her closer to the bridge's railing.

"At least tell me why you did it," Susannah said, trying to stall for more time as she used her free hand to reach into her purse, hoping to find something to hit him or distract him with. "You claimed you loved Elsbeth. How could you love someone and then murder them?"

"She didn't love me back. She *wouldn't* love me back."

"So you killed her?" Her fingers closed around her keys. She remembered a self-defense course she'd taken at the local Y that advised using keys to strike at an attacker's eyes. But first she had to get the keys out of her purse without him seeing her.

"That's right. If I couldn't have her, then no one could."

They were almost at the bridge's railing. "What are you going to do now?" she demanded, the fear in her voice very real.

"What do you think, Mrs. Wilder? If that is your real name."

"What do you mean?"

"I mean that Mr. Whitaker had me telegraph your supposed dear friend Althea Hall of New York City. She telegraphed back this morning that she'd never heard of either Kane or Susannah Wilder. We also telegraphed the jeweler, the one you claimed supposedly made that necklace for you." Gordon reached out to flick the necklace insultingly. "And he also denied ever hearing of either of you. I would remind you, Mrs. Whoever-you-are, that you don't have much time left on this earth. So you had better tell me now—who are you?"

"A friend of Elsbeth's." Susannah sensed her presence around her in the thickly swirling fog. "She brought me here to solve her murder."

"What are you talking about?"

"I'm not a friend of Althea Hall's. I'm her great-granddaughter."

"That's impossible!"

"Not with the help of a ghost. Elsbeth's ghost. She's here now."

Startled, Gordon loosened his grip momentarily. Seizing her chance, Susannah grabbed her keys, inadvertently yanking on the personal alarm as she did so. Its shrill sound pierced the night.

Kane heard the noise and recognized it for what it was—a device from his own time. "Susannah!" he shouted into the thick mist. "Where are you?"

The fog displaced the noise, muffling it and giving him false readings.

He shouted her name again.

"Here! Kane, I'm here! Help me!"

Susannah's struggle with Gordon was hindered by the fact that he'd heard her alarm go off. At first, he'd stepped away from her to cover his ears. Freed of his hold, Susannah had turned to run, only to trip over the hem of her red velvet dress.

Gordon's hold on her arm had prevented her from falling flat on her face, but now his grip was tighter than ever as he dragged her toward the railing once again, stepping on the wailing alarm in the process. When that didn't stop it, he kicked it over the edge of the bridge. The noise abruptly stopped as the alarm hit the water below. He swiftly grabbed her purse and heaved it into the river. "You're next," he said.

"Kane!" Susannah shrieked, as she dug in her heels.

And then Kane was there. Coming out of the white fog like a legendary hero of old, his shout of fury was like an ancient Viking battle cry. He aimed straight for Gordon, hitting him in the back, just at the kidneys, with his shoulder.

For one perilous second, Susannah teetered on the edge of the railing. She felt herself falling, her horrified gaze staring into the murky darkness below, before a hand grabbed her and yanked her back to safety.

It was Kane. She clutched his shoulders as he briefly hugged her. Looking over her shoulder, she cried out a warning. "Look out, Kane, he's got a knife!"

Shoving her aside, Kane pivoted, turning on his heel and ducking as Gordon slashed air instead of muscle.

"What's the matter, Gordo?" Kane taunted, his hands held out in a universal come-get-me gesture. "Feeling the heat, are you? Starting to panic a little?"

Gordon lashed out again, this time coming closer than Kane felt real comfortable with. Damn it, where was Oliver?

"So why'd you do it, Gordo? Why did you shove Elsbeth down those stairs?"

"I already told you."

"Not me. You didn't tell me. Must have been someone else. You're getting confused, Gordo. Does that happen to you a lot, lately? I'll bet it does. Because you're definitely a few cards short of a full deck, aren't you, Gordo?"

"Stop calling me that!" Gordon yelled, his face turning red. He struck out with the knife again, this time missing Kane by a goodly distance.

"Your stress is showing, Gordo. Maybe they'll go easy on you. After all, you're not sane. Is that why you did it?"

"I killed Elsbeth because I loved her," Gordon shouted. "And I'm not going to jail for it!"

"Did you hear that, Oliver?" Kane yelled out into the fog, praying the detective had arrived by now. Susannah stood in the background; he could see her shivering.

"I'm not falling for that old trick," Gordon scoffed.

"I heard it," Oliver confirmed from the mist. "You'd do best to turn yourself in, Mr. Stevens," the detective called out, his voice getting nearer by the second. "The authorities will look on you more favorably if you do. You know the law, Mr. Stevens."

Turning his attention back to Susannah, Gordon shouted, "This is all your fault. It's because of you that I'm in all this trouble!"

Quick as a flash, he ran toward her, his knife raised.

Kane managed to knock the knife from the law clerk's hand but couldn't stop the other man from grabbing Susannah.

"Let her go," Kane gritted.

The gleam in Gordon Stevens's eyes was fiendish as he yelled in a shrill voice, "I'm not going to prison!"

"You don't have much choice in the matter," Oliver said as he joined Kane.

Kane's heart was in his throat. He couldn't rush Gordon now; the man was perched on top of the railing, and he had a tight grip on Susannah's arm. If Gordon fell or jumped, he'd take Susannah with him. She'd already almost ended up in the river once, tonight.

"I have a choice," Gordon shouted at them. "And I'm taking it. I'm not going to jail. I'd rather end my life in the river."

"Fine by me," Kane said, his voice deadly. "But you're not taking Susannah with you."

"You can't stop me." Squinting into the mist, Gordon suddenly gasped. "Elsbeth!"

Kane saw his chance and he took it. Leaping forward, he took hold of Susannah's other arm, yanking her from Gordon's grasp just as the law clerk slipped and toppled into the Savannah River.

"It'll be all right," Kane whispered soothingly as he rocked Susannah in his arms.

"He was going to kill me," Susannah said, her voice shaking almost as much as she was.

Echoes of the violence and fear she'd just lived through continued to reverberate through her, as her mind flashed by an instant replay of all that had just occurred.

In the distance she was vaguely aware of Oliver talking to uniformed officers. The police. But she preferred to keep her attention focused on Kane, the warmth of his lips brushing her temple as he murmured reassurances to her, the tender way he held her in his arms, the gentleness of his hands.

When she finally did lift her head from his shoulder the first thing she noticed was that the thick mist was lifting with a mysterious and unnatural suddenness, leaving her wondering if the thick pea-souper had been a natural phenomenon or a bit of ghostly magic devised by Elsbeth.

"The fog is clearing up," she said.

"Are you sure you're all right?" he asked yet again.

She nodded. "He threw my purse over the bridge," she said.

"I know. It will be okay," he murmured soothingly, running his hand over her cheek.

"No, it won't. What if that purse shows up again and they find my credit cards and everything else in there? I could mess up history."

"I doubt that."

"Okay, then how do I explain the loss to the credit-card company? Tell the customer-service rep that some Victorian maniac disposed of my purse and its contents into the Savannah River a hundred and eleven years ago? That will go over big, I'm sure!"

Seeing Oliver approaching them, Kane made no reply, but did gently squeeze her shoulder in warning.

"Good news. First off, may I say that I'm greatly relieved that you are all right, Mrs. Wilder," Oliver said.

"I think that after what we've been through you may call me Susannah now," she replied.

"Yes, well, one of the police officers found your bag. It was dangling from one of the bridge's support beams below and we managed to retrieve it for you."

"Thank heavens!" She snatched it from him and hugged it to her bosom. Looking down at the dirty smudge the bag made on her velvet dress, she sighed. "This dress is never going to recover."

"I've arranged for a carriage to take you back to your boardinghouse," Oliver said. "I'll just tell the police you're leaving."

Once he was gone, Susannah took a few steps away from Kane, only to almost trip over something. "What?" Looking down, she saw the gleam of her keys. She quickly bent down to pick them up. The alarm must have come loose from the key chain when Gordon stepped on it and in the scuffle the keys had been kicked aside. She gripped them in her hand, the metal biting into her palm.

Kane gently undid her clenched fist, took the keys and put them in her purse for her. Zipping the bag closed, he put an arm around her. "Come on. You've got your bag and your keys and most important, you've got your life. I'll take you back to the boardinghouse now."

"No." Susannah lifted her head as if listening for something...or someone. "No, we have to go to the Whitaker house."

"At this time of night?" Oliver said, having just rejoined them. "Whatever for? I can assure you that Mr. Whitaker knew nothing of his law clerk's activities either here this evening or the night that Elsbeth Whitaker was killed."

"Did you ever find out who Whitaker was meeting in the cemetery that night?"

Oliver nodded. "Indeed I did. A private investigator. It seems that Mr. Whitaker was having second thoughts and suspicions of his own about Mrs. Hilton. Like you, he thought she might have committed the dastardly deed."

"I never thought she did it," Susannah denied. "I had a feeling—"

"The same feeling you're getting now about going to the Whitaker house?" Kane asked.

She nodded. She sensed Elsbeth's presence so very strongly. And with it came an urgency that it was now or never if they wanted to return home again.

"I've learned to trust your feelings," Kane told her.

This was news to Susannah. "You have?"

He nodded. Turning to Oliver, he said, "We're going to need your help. Do you think you can help get us into the Whitaker house tonight?"

"I believe Mr. Whitaker is still at the police station giving his statement."

"We don't need to speak to Mr. Whitaker."

"Then why are you going to his house?"

"It's a long story. I'll tell you in the carriage on the way there."

Once they were safely ensconced inside, Oliver said, "Does this have something to do with your being from . . . France?"

"We're not from France. We're from the future. Elsbeth Whitaker's ghost brought us back in time to solve the mystery of her death," Kane said bluntly.

Oliver took the news well.

"I must say, you're acting very calm about all this," Kane noted.

"I had my suspicions that more than an ocean separated the two of you from all the rest of us," Oliver responded dryly. "And that watch of yours, Kane. If *that* didn't come from the future, I don't know what would."

"I told you not to wear that watch," Susannah reminded him. "It was bound to get us into trouble sooner or later."

"It got us into some serious difficulties this evening. It seems that one of your husband's poker-playing friends had his heart set on obtaining that watch for himself. He hired a thug to accompany him in an ambush as Kane and I stood outside the boardinghouse, attempting to hail a cab and come to your rescue."

"Were you hurt?" she immediately asked Kane.

"No. It was nothing but a nuisance."

"If you'd arrived any later..." Susannah's voice trailed off as a shudder shook her body.

Giving Oliver an impatient look, Kane hugged her reassuringly. "But we did arrive in time. And we'll arrive at the Whitaker house in time, too."

"In time to do what?" Oliver asked.

"To go back to where we belong," Kane replied.

"This really is most amazing. So people in your time travel through the centuries as if visiting a neighboring city?"

"No, I wouldn't say that," Kane said wryly.

"It is still an experimental procedure, then? You are scientists, perhaps?"

"No, we're definitely not scientists," Susannah answered. "My real name is Susannah Hall and I'm related to a friend of Elsbeth's—"

"Althea Hall. Yes, I had heard that Mr. Whitaker had telegraphed her and she had never heard of you. Now it makes sense, of course. But at the time I could not fathom how you'd gotten such an exact replica of the much-talked-about garnet jewelry set."

"I inherited it," Susannah said.

Oliver nodded, as if he'd placed another piece in a complicated puzzle.

"We still need to come up with a plan to get into the Whitaker house," Kane declared. "Got any ideas?"

Oliver nodded, his attention returning to the matter at hand. "It would be best if we go to the back door. I've gotten to know the cook fairly well during my investigation. I will strive to distract the good woman while the two of you slip inside. As I recall, the back door opens outward, which would make it easier for you to hide behind."

"Sounds good to me."

"Excellent. Once I've distracted the cook by asking her something about the case, perhaps, and getting her to step outside, the two of you should make your way around the door and into the kitchen."

"Right," Kane agreed. "I guess this is goodbye, then," he added as their carriage stopped in the side street beside the house.

"We can never repay you for all your help," Susannah said, giving the detective a hug.

"She's right. We owe you big-time." Kane shook Oliver's hand, pressing all of the remaining nineteenth-century money he had into the detective's palm. "It's not enough, I know. I can't think of a way to repay you— Wait a second! Sure, I can. If you're interested in doing some investing, I'd recommend looking into the inventions of Thomas Edison and Henry Ford."

"Don't forget Alexander Graham Bell," Susannah added as Kane helped her out of the carriage.

"You mean that telephone idea actually makes a go of it?" Oliver asked.

"Big-time."

"I wonder what else is in store for the next hundred years," Oliver murmured.

Susannah stood close to Kane behind the shelter of the door as Oliver expertly drew the cook outside to view a supposed footprint near the garden path. The moon was bright enough to provide light and it cast a shadow as she and Kane slipped around the door and into the kitchen. They'd never been to this part of the house before and were completely unfamiliar with the layout.

Kane opened one door only to discover that it led to a pantry. The sound of Hayward Whitaker's voice sent them scurrying inside.

Susannah held her breath, sighing in relief at the sound of Oliver calling Hayward outside, as well.

"Come on," Kane whispered, taking her hand and tugging her after him. "We've got to get upstairs before they catch us here."

"Wait," she said. "I think this other door leads from the pantry to the dining room and then the parlor. Once we're there, we know where the stairs are. That's where the party was last time we were here, remember?"

Kane led the way as they hurried through the empty rooms and up the curved staircase. The closer they got to the third floor, the more Susannah was filled with a magical sense of anticipation.

As she had that first time, she felt drawn forward. From the top landing, she could see the flickering candlelight.

"Damn, there's someone in there," Kane muttered.

"No, it's all right," Susannah said. "Come on."

As she and Kane stepped into the room, the candlelight was infused with an ethereal blue light. In the midst of that glow, Susannah could clearly see a woman standing there.

It was Elsbeth! Gone were the sad eyes portrayed in the painting; Elsbeth was gently smiling and her expression was that of a woman finally at peace. She mouthed the words, *Thank you,* and held out her hand.

As before, Susannah was drawn toward the vision, moving closer, closer... almost touching Elsbeth's outstretched hand as the glow increased until it was almost blinding. Then the room abruptly went pitch-black and the tranquil silence was shattered by a sharp crash and a woman's scream.

# Eleven

---

"**S**usannah!" Crying out her name and cursing under his breath, Kane reached into his pants pocket and removed a book of twentieth-century matches. Striking a match and holding it up, he saw that the room was no longer furnished—the walls had been ripped down to the bare studs and the room was littered with construction materials.

"Susannah, where are you?"

"I'm right here," Susannah said.

Relieved to see her, Kane let the match burn out and took her in his arms. "Are you all right?"

"Yes." Her voice was shaky, but her hold on him was tight. They were back! They'd made it. And she and Kane were going to make it as a couple, too. She felt more confident of that now than she ever had before.

"What happened?" Kane asked.

"I walked into an empty bucket with a paintbrush in it."

"You made enough noise to raise the dead."

"Did you see her? Elsbeth was here."

Kane made no reply; instead he released her. "Come on, let's get out of here." Lighting another match, he led her through the maze of junk stored in the room.

Walking through the doorway, Susannah noted, "Look, the mirror is gone." She pointed to the third-story window.

They'd just reached the top of the stairs, when a tour guide met them on her way up. "I thought I heard a noise up here. This area is off-limits to visitors," she said with a disapproving frown. "Most of the people from the publishing party have gone already. We're closing up."

"What day is it?" Kane asked.

"It's Wednesday night, although since it will be midnight any moment, technically it will be Thursday soon."

Kane and Susannah exchanged a silent look as they simultaneously realized that—although they'd been in the past for two weeks—it was still the same evening here as when they'd left, albeit a few hours later. But how could that be?

"I really must ask you to leave. We're closing up now," the guide reminded them.

"One thing before we go," Susannah said. "Would you please tell me about the woman in this portrait?"

The guide's curtness melted some at the request. "The woman's name was Elsbeth Whitaker and hers is a tragic story. She was murdered by a besotted admirer, her husband's law clerk, who later killed himself in a fit of guilt. He threw himself off a bridge and drowned in the Savannah River."

Susannah felt a sad sense of completion. Their mission had been successful. They'd cleared Elsbeth's name from the suicide charges and changed history in a small way.

Seeing their interest, the tour guide added, "The mystery was solved by Oliver Ogilvie, Savannah's most famous detective. Mr. Ogilvie went on to become quite wealthy through his wise investments in the new technologies of that era. While Mr. Ogilvie didn't have any children of his own, his adopted son Michael went on to become a prominent citizen. Indeed, he was the police chief for much of his later life. His family is still active in civic activities here.''

Susannah and Kane looked at each other and in unison said, ''Mikey?''

''Excuse me?'' the guide said.

''Nothing,'' Susannah hurriedly stated. ''Thank you so much for telling us Elsbeth's story.''

''Unfortunately the Victorian era wasn't a very interesting period in Savannah's illustrious history. Actually, it was a rather boring time.''

''Oh, I wouldn't say that,'' Susannah murmured. ''It wasn't boring at all!''

Susannah walked out of the Whitaker house with Kane at her side and was immediately struck by the heat and the noise. The park across the street was more brightly illuminated than it had been in 1884. And cars were passing by on asphalt streets. Traffic wasn't heavy at that time of night, but after being away from automobiles, the smell of exhaust and diesel fumes was definitely noticeable.

Things got even more overwhelming as they walked the short distance to the main thoroughfare. Where Susannah had once questioned Mrs. Hilton in the dress shop, there were now abandoned buildings with the fronts boarded up. Those stores that remained had thick security bars across the windows. A homeless man slept on a doorstep nearby.

It was a hell of a homecoming.

Kane didn't say a word as he quickly caught a cab that was fortuitously passing by.

*Fortuitously,* Susannah thought as she got in the back seat of the cab, struggling to slide over the ripped vinyl. No one used that word anymore. Words were shorter now. Clipped sound bites.

''Where to?'' the cabbie asked Kane as he got in.

Kane named a hotel by the waterfront. ''What hotel are you staying in?'' he asked her.

The fact that he didn't even know where she was staying in Savannah made Susannah realize how little Kane really knew about her.

"I'm staying there, as well," she quietly replied.

She could sense him retreating farther and farther away from her during the tense cab ride back to their hotel. He stayed on his side of the cab, not touching her and not speaking.

This was *not* a good sign, she noted, trying not to panic. She hadn't seen this reaction coming at all. Normally her instincts were good at warning her about impending trouble.

Okay, so they hadn't been the strongest when dealing with Gordon Stevens, but she had known that Mrs. Hilton wasn't the murderer. So her instincts hadn't disappeared altogether.

But with Kane they seemed to be off kilter, like a compass placed next to a magnetic source.

All she knew was there was a definite awkwardness on Kane's part as they returned to their hotel. Using his stash of modern money, he paid for the cab.

Feeling just as awkward, Susannah automatically dug into her purse to pay her share.

Kane waved her off. Not looking at her, he curtly said, "I'll see you."

Standing in the air-conditioned lobby, she watched him walk away from her and felt utterly bereft. Telling herself not to be so sensitive, she headed for the bank of elevators. He was standing there still, waiting for one. But, once again, he didn't say a word to her. The gulf of silence threatened to drown her.

"Are you okay?" she finally asked.

"I don't know how to answer that question," he replied, keeping his eyes on the elevator floor-display light. She could almost hear his sigh of relief when the elevator finally arrived. He couldn't wait to get away from her. He stepped right in. She didn't.

Seeing the impatient look he gave her, she murmured unsteadily, "You go ahead. I'll catch the next one."

"Look, it's just been a hell of a few weeks, or hours," Kane said abruptly. "I think we both need some time to ourselves to adjust."

A second later the cold metal doors closed in her face, and the chasm in her heart split wide open.

*Time to ourselves. To adjust.* Kane's words kept repeating themselves over and over again as Susannah sat on the edge of her hotel bed, the tears running down her face as she removed the rented velvet dress. She'd been right. The outfit wouldn't recover from the workout she'd put it through. And neither would she.

She hadn't known it was possible to hurt this deeply. As she wiped the tears away with her hand, she wondered if the pain was doubled by the fact that she hadn't seen the blow coming and therefore hadn't been able to brace herself. When they'd come back to their own time and Kane had taken her in his arms, she'd been so sure that things would work out between them. Instead, everything had been shattered just when she'd thought she'd found happiness, had it in her hand. But it seemed destined to remain out of reach.

And so did Kane. The thought of being without him left a vengefully and inconsolably deep ache, as if a fiery sword had been driven into her very soul. His cold words had struck home and scored a direct hit, leaving no embers of hope behind.

As she stepped into the shower, she was very much aware of the fact that Kane had never said he loved her. With numb passivity, she bleakly reminded herself that he'd never even said he believed her about not having had an affair with his brother, either. Standing under the stinging spray of water, she knew there was no washing away the anguish lodged inside her breast.

Working on automatic, she got ready for bed. She was exhausted. Kane had been correct about one thing—it *had* been a hell of a few weeks, or hours—depending on which century they'd been in. Either way, she'd been through enough to last her three lifetimes.

Her body was ready for sleep but her mind refused to shut down, trying to make sense out of what had happened, brooding over the conflicting impressions she'd picked up from Kane. Remembering his tenderness when he'd made love with her, the way he'd come to her rescue on that bridge tonight, risking his own life to save hers. Closing her eyes, she felt the intensity of his embrace as he'd held her and rocked her in his arms, the gentleness with which he'd brushed her hair away from her face. Those weren't the actions of a man who didn't care. And then there was his concern for her safety less than two hours ago when the room at the Whitaker house had gone pitch-black and he'd lit a match to see her.

He'd lit a fire in her soul and Susannah used those flames to fan her anger. Was she going to sit around like a simpering schoolgirl and bemoan her fate? Or was she going to take things into her own hands and do something about the situation? Because something definitely didn't make sense here.

Turning on the light and sitting up in bed, she said, "Oh, hell, what have I got to lose?"

Kane was all set to ignore the knock on his door. Looking at his watch, he saw it was almost two in the morning. He hadn't ordered room service and he certainly wasn't expecting company. Looking at the watch gave him flashbacks to Oliver and the rest of the nineteenth-century people he'd met. "You call that a watch?" J.P. had said to him at the poker game.

The knock on his door came again, and with enough persistence to convince Kane that the late-night visitor wasn't going away. Peering through the peephole, he saw it was Susannah. She was wearing some kind of baggy T-shirt over matching dusty blue knit pants. Her hair was still damp and piled up on top of her head with one of those elastic things so popular now. She looked disheveled, disgruntled, and mad as hell. She also looked heart-stoppingly beautiful.

He opened the door.

Not waiting for an invitation, Susannah marched into his room and glared at him. "Look, I'm not going to beat around the bush, here. I'm not going to politely pretend that nothing happened between us. I'm going to get right to the point. What are your feelings for me?" she demanded. "Because I happen to have been foolish enough—no, make that brave enough—to have fallen in love with you. And I'm woman enough to tell you that, even though you haven't told me your feelings yet." She took a gulp of much-needed air before continuing. "And while we're being direct here, I want to know once and for all if you finally believe me when I swear that I didn't have an affair with your brother."

"I don't know what the situation is with my brother—" Kane began.

He *didn't* believe her. Susannah was stricken. She'd risked everything to bare her soul to him and the huge gamble had backfired right in her face. She didn't want to hear any more. She just wanted to get out of there. Pivoting, she blindly reached for the doorknob.

"Wait!" Kane said, grabbing hold of her shoulders to stop her in her tracks. "You're not listening to me," he gently scolded her. "You've kind of made a habit of that. What I was saying is that while I don't know what the situation is with my brother, I *do* believe you. I no longer believe you had an affair with him. You've always been honest with me," he noted, brushing a loose tendril of her dark wavy hair away from her big brown eyes. "Sometimes painfully so."

Susannah gulped back the tears. "You believe me?"

He nodded. "I don't know why my brother said what he did, but I no longer believe him. I trust you. And I love you."

"Then why did you . . . ?"

"Back away from you? I panicked," he admitted. "Jumping centuries in a single bound makes it hard to put things in perspective, you know? I told you before, I've always had a logical approach to life. An explanation for everything. I haven't had much experience with faith and hope. Until you came into my life." Reaching out, he cupped her cheek in his hand, his touch conveying so much tenderness that Susannah felt tears coming into her eyes. This time they were tears of relief.

Kane kissed them away. His mouth gently skimmed her eyelids, her cheeks, the delicate pulse at her temple. She tugged him lower, meeting his lips with hers and greeting them with unspoken joy. Their kiss was both an exploration and a celebration.

He tugged her T-shirt over her head and tossed it over his shoulder. He was surprised to discover that beneath the baggy attire, she was wearing an incredibly sexy and slinky purple satin chemise nightie. Grinning a gambler's daredevil grin, he murmured, "You know, there are advantages to being back in the twentieth century."

His hotly appreciative gaze followed the line of what little material there was. The nightie only went to midthigh and was held up by spaghetti straps, which he took delight in nudging off her bare shoulders with his teeth.

The rake of his strong teeth over her bare skin sent shivers down her spine. When one strap slid down her arm, he lifted his head and gave her a steamy look. "Take down your hair for me," he whispered.

She lifted her arms to remove the fabric-covered elastic band. Her movement thrust her breasts upward. Unable to resist, Kane lowered his head to nibble at her flesh through the satiny fabric. Susannah purred his name as her hair fell to her shoulders and her hands reached for him. Sliding her fingers through his silky dark brown hair, she felt a drugging warmth sweeping through her.

Her right hand cupped his nape while she lifted her left to slide the remaining strap off her shoulder. Now the curve of her breasts and his lips were the only thing keeping the material in place. As soon as Kane realized that, he tugged on the hem of the nightie. The friction of the satin moving against her nipples was enough to make her sink her fingers into his shoulders.

She wanted no barriers between them. So she got rid of his T-shirt as efficiently as he'd done hers. Only now did she even register what he was actually wearing. "You look good in jeans," she murmured appreciatively, even as she set about unfastening them. "Ah, but you look even better out of them."

Kane's smile was slow and filled with promise as he stepped out of the jeans before sweeping her into his arms and carrying her to bed, where the remaining bits of underwear were quickly discarded.

"Another good thing about being back in the twentieth century is the fact that I've got more condoms," he muttered.

"Perhaps you'd care to model one for me?" she inquired seductively.

"Inside out or right side out?" he wickedly returned.

"Whichever you prefer."

Once he was sheathed in the latex condom, he reached out to touch her with dark intimacy, brushing his thumb against her crisp curls, searching out and finding the secret nub of her pleasure. The expanse of his reach was such that he could continue his erotic seduction while slowly sliding his finger into her slick passage, verifying her readiness for him.

"It's been another hundred and eleven years since we've made love," she managed to gasp even as she tugged his hips down to hers. "I don't think we need to wait any longer."

He came to her in slow doses, his thick shaft poised far enough inside to tease her with the incredibly sensual friction. "As I recall, this felt right to you."

She grinned with brazen feminine satisfaction. "Ah, you chose inside out!"

"I take it . . . ah . . ." Kane groaned as she gently clenched around his arousal. "I take it . . . you approve?" His voice was gritty with desire.

She showed him how much—with actions not with words. The buildup of ecstasy was slow and spiraling, sending her spinning like a leaf in a whirlwind, ever upward, from one plateau to the next until she reached the very apex of passion. The experience was intense and primitive, timeless and evolving.

Whether in this century or the last, when Kane made love to her the result was the same. Ecstasy drenched her senses, spilling over from one rippling motion to the next, growing and expanding into sharply blissful contractions.

"I can't . . . wait . . ." he gasped.

She showed him there was no need to wait, reaching her completion just as he started his.


Susannah was only hazily aware of Kane reaching toward the bedside table for something. Thinking he was reaching for the package of condoms, she languidly murmured, "Again? So soon?"

He tore off a sheet of paper from the notepad the hotel supplied and handed it to her.

"What's this?"

"An apology. I was working on it when you came pounding on my door. Remember how when we first met at the convention center you said you expected a written apology from me for thinking you'd had an affair with my brother?"

Blinking away the tears at the words he'd written, she looked up at him. "I don't know what to say," she whispered.

"That's okay. Because I've got something to say. Marry me."

This time her blink was one of total surprise. "Marry you?"

"That's right. What do you say?"

Before she could reply, the phone rang. Susannah automatically reached for it, picking up the receiver before remembering this wasn't her room, it was Kane's. Without speaking into the receiver, she immediately handed it over to him.

She could tell by the tension in his face and his body that it was his brother calling. Susannah braced herself for the worst.

Seeing Susannah's defensive body language, Kane reached out to brush her cheek with the back of his hand as he mouthed, *It'll be okay.*

"I've been trying to reach you, Kane," his brother was saying, his voice frantic. "There's something I have to tell you. I . . . I've done some serious soul-searching and I have a confession to make. I had no idea you'd meet Ms. Hall down there in Savannah and confront her. . . . Ann told me. . . . It was a lie, Kane. I never had an affair with her. I don't know why I said I did. . . ." Chuck's laugh was that of a man close to tears. "Maybe because . . . because I've always been intimidated by all your success. And maybe because I wanted to be a man of the world, myself. So I made up this fantasy about Susannah. I don't know if you noticed, big brother, but she is a beautiful woman."

"I noticed," Kane said quietly.

"Yeah, well, she never seemed to notice me as anything other than an intern. I just kept building things in my head. It wasn't like I was in love with her or anything, it was just this fantasy to make me feel more important, you know? Anyway, I've talked things over with Ann, and I've agreed to get some counseling to see if our marriage can be saved."

"I think that's a good idea."

"Yeah, well, anyway . . . uh, I just wanted to say that I'm sorry I dragged you into this mess, bro," Chuck said. "Who knows, maybe you and Susannah will get along, after all."

"I'd say that's a sure bet," Kane replied before saying his goodbyes and hanging up the phone.

"What did he want?" Susannah asked.

"To set the record straight," Kane said. "He confessed that he'd made the story up about the two of you. And he's agreed to get some counseling to help save his marriage."

"That's good news."

"Speaking of good news, I'm still waiting to hear some from you. I asked you an important question—the most important question in my life—and you still haven't answered."

Trying hard to be logical, Susannah said, "You do realize that in *this* time zone we've only known each other twenty-four hours."

"We spent two weeks living together in 1884," Kane countered. "How many other couples have that kind of background to build on?"

"Still, two weeks isn't a real long time...."

"Funny how time flies when you're having fun," Kane noted with a wicked grin. "And when you're in love. We can work out all the details later. Just say yes, you will marry me."

She did, with words and with actions.

*     *     *     *     *

**SILHOUETTE**

*Desire*

# COMING NEXT MONTH

## ARIZONA HEAT
### Jennifer Greene

Paxton Moore was happy with his life just the way it was until Kansas McClellan barged into town, asking him for help in her search for her missing brother. Why were the sultry days—and hot nights—suddenly getting too steamy for comfort?

## COWBOY HOMECOMING
### Pamela Ingrahm

When Steve Williams went back to the old family ranch, he was shocked to find a beautiful blonde sitting at his kitchen table claiming the land was hers. All Steve wanted was solitude, not the irresistible Tegan McReed!

## ONCE IN A BLUE MOON
### Kristin James

Michael Traynor was back, sexier than ever. But Isabelle Gray was no longer the lovesick teenager who had once fallen into his bed. Could she keep hidden the ten-year-old secret she'd harboured since he left?

**SILHOUETTE**

*Desire*

# COMING NEXT MONTH

## REBEL LOVE
### Jackie Merritt

Cass Whitfield had been devastated when rebel Gard Sterling hadn't remembered the passion-filled night they'd spent together. Could Gard now convince her that he wasn't the same bad boy who hurt her all those years ago?

## ANGELS AND ELVES
### Joan Elliott Pickart

*Man of the Month*

The most important thing in confirmed bachelor Forrest MacAllister's busy life was his family. Until he saw sexy Jillian Jones-Jenkins, who had him thinking about things he'd never considered before—like brides and babies and happily ever after...

## WHATEVER COMES
### Lass Small

Reporter Amabel Clayton was furious when people assumed she'd slept with a man to get a story. Particularly when the man was elusive rock star Sean Morant. Talented, sensuous and sexy...he was *definitely* off limits!

# COMING NEXT MONTH FROM

 **SILHOUETTE**

## Sensation
*A thrilling mix of passion, adventure and drama*

**MARRIED BY A THREAD** Kia Cochrane
**CAITLIN'S GUARDIAN ANGEL** Marie Ferrarella
**AN OFFICER AND A GENTLEMAN** Rachel Lee
**A MAN LIKE SMITH** Marilyn Pappano

## Intrigue
*Danger, deception and desire*

**WINTER'S EDGE** Anne Stuart
**BEHIND THE MASK** Joanna Wayne
**UNSPOKEN CONFESSIONS** Kelsey Roberts
**THE SUSPECT GROOM** Cassie Miles

## Special Edition
*Satisfying romances packed with emotion*

**MAGGIE'S DAD** Diana Palmer
**MORGAN'S SON** Lindsay McKenna
**CHILD OF MINE** Jennifer Mikels
**THE DADDY QUEST** Celeste Hamilton
**LOGAN'S BRIDE** Christine Flynn
**BRAVE HEART** Brittany Young

# Name that Song

How would you like to win a year's supply of sophisticated and deeply emotional romances? Well, you can and they're free! Simply solve the puzzle below and send your completed entry to us by 30th September 1996. The first five correct entries picked after the closing date will each win a years supply of Silhouette Special Edition novels (six books every month—worth over £160).

*Please turn over for details of how to enter* 👉

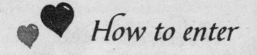 *How to enter*

To solve our puzzle...first circle eight well known girls names hidden in the grid. Then unscramble the remaining letters to reveal the title of a well-known song (five words).

When you have written the song title in the space provided below, don't forget to fill in your name and address, pop this page into an envelope (you don't need a stamp) and post it today! Hurry—competition ends 30th September 1996.

**Silhouette Song Puzzle**
**FREEPOST**
**Croydon**
**Surrey**
**CR9 3WZ**

Song Title: _____

Are you a Reader Service Subscriber?  Yes ❑   No ❑

Ms/Mrs/Miss/Mr _____

Address _____

_____

_____ Postcode _____

One application per household.

You may be mailed with other offers from other reputable companies as a result of this application. If you would prefer not to receive such offers, please tick box.  ❑

COMP196
C